"WHAT WAS THAT NOISE?"

We stared at the window, which Charlene opened when we had first arrived at the summer house. Then she said softly, "Turn out the light, Marjorie."

The light switch was on the wall by the door, the gouged-up door. My fingers flew to it, and the room was instantly dark. I heard Charlene's chair move across the floor as she stood up.

Together we huddled by the window, staring into the woods . . .

Something moved between the trees. Something large. No squirrel or rabbit or dog. Something much larger than that. Something as large as a man.

Someone w̶̶̶̶̶̶̶̶̶̶̶̶̶̶̶̶̶̶̶̶̶̶̶̶ rom the nightfal

WHERE EVIL IS

CAROL BEACH YORK

AN ARCHWAY PAPERBACK
Published by POCKET BOOKS • NEW YORK

AN ARCHWAY PAPERBACK *Original*

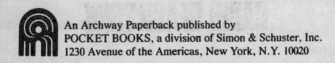

An Archway Paperback published by
POCKET BOOKS, a division of Simon & Schuster, Inc.
1230 Avenue of the Americas, New York, N.Y. 10020

ISBN: 0-671-64372-X

First Archway Paperback printing September 1987

10 9 8 7 6 5 4 3 2 1

AN ARCHWAY PAPERBACK and colophon are
registered trademarks of Simon & Schuster, Inc.

Printed in the U.S.A.

IL 7+

WHERE EVIL IS

Chapter One

THINGS ARE NOT ALWAYS WHAT THEY seem. I have learned that lesson now, and I will remember it well.

It was last summer in August, I was almost sixteen, and I was invited to spend a few weeks with my cousin Charlene. She was married—her married name Charlene Kensington. That has a glamorous sound, doesn't it? And Charlene fit the name; she was a real beauty. A slender body, violet-blue eyes with sweeping lashes, silky, yellow hair the color of every girl's dreams. Certainly of mine.

She had grown up in a brown frame house about a block away from my house in Sanderville, which is in Indiana. You may not have heard of it because it's a small town. Our road signs say

WHERE EVIL IS

WELCOME TO SANDERVILLE
Population: 6,435
HAVE A NICE DAY

Charlene is ten years older than I am, and she often baby-sat me when she was in high school and I was just coping with kindergarten and first grade. When she went away to college, I always looked forward to her homecomings. She brought an aura of enchanted worlds back to me, and I longed for my own college days to begin—they seemed so far away.

After college she went to live in Chicago, where she worked in an advertising agency. Her mother and father sold the brown frame house in Sanderville and went out to Arizona to live.

I always felt sort of sad when I went by the house after that. Strangers were living there, and Aunt Kate, Uncle Gerald, and Charlene were far away. I remembered a lot of good times in that brown frame house. Christmas Eves. Thanksgiving dinners. My mom always said Aunt Kate and Uncle Gerald spoiled Charlene and gave her everything she asked for—which didn't sound like such a bad deal to me. Anyway, they were gone, and I never went inside their house again.

Eventually, about a year after she went to live in Chicago, Charlene met David. David Kensington, a distinguished-sounding name, which suited him as well as Charlene's name suited her. I think names are important—and full of clues about a person.

Unfortunately my name doesn't sound special, or glamorous, or mysterious. "Marjorie" sounds like somebody who gets good grades and doesn't have a lot of boyfriends. Which is true of me. I think anybody could hear my name and just *know* I'm sort of plump and brown-eyed and not very tall.

When Charlene and David were married, Charlene gave up her job at the advertising agency. They bought a house in an exclusive suburb called Larrimore Hills, about an hour's drive from Chicago. That was where I was invited to visit. Charlene and David, who had been married about three years, also had a summer cottage in a resort area in Michigan, and Charlene said we would spend some time there during my visit. I was thrilled.

I would go to Larrimore Hills on Am-Trak, a four-hour ride.

I arrived there on a warm Sunday afternoon, laden with suitcases and full of joy, to begin a series of days that were to be the strangest and in the end the most frightening I had ever experienced.

Charlene and I sat on the patio together as that first afternoon drew to a close. She had shown me through the house, which was as gorgeous as I had known it would be. Then we had come out to the patio with glasses of iced tea.

She was as beautiful as ever—more beautiful. She was sitting in a white wicker chair with a curving, dramatically high back that rose above her head. I thought she looked like the royal lady of some exotic estate in India. Ice tinkled in her glass as she gazed contentedly across the garden. I could see how much she loved it.

"Those are lilac bushes along the east end," she told me. "They're *so* beautiful in the spring."

"I love lilacs," I said eagerly. Anything Charlene liked, I liked. I had adored her ever since I could remember.

That afternoon she was wearing pink silk slacks and a matching halter top, mauve eye shadow, and antique silver earrings. Her ears were pierced, and the earrings were the long, dangling kind that shimmered and caught the light when she moved her head. Her blond hair was loose, casual, brushing her shoulders.

I was dazed with joy at actually being there. Everything was wonderful: the house, the patio, the sunny garden, the glisten of sunlight on the spray as the sprinkler whirred by the lilac bushes and Charlene sipped her tea.

Her husband David joined us before long. He had been playing golf, and he apologized to me for not being with Charlene to meet my train.

"I'm sorry I wasn't here when you arrived. I thought I would be."

David was older than Charlene—about forty, I think. He was rather reserved and formal, and I at once felt shy. I had liked it better when it was just Charlene and me sitting on the patio.

"How was Am-Trak?" David settled himself in a

chair opposite me and stretched his legs out in front of him. He was one of those tall men who has to find someplace to stretch out his long legs. His clothes were casual but expensive, the kind of weekend clothes worn by a man who has succeeded. He had dark hair just graying at the temples, and dark eyes which reflected a serious nature. I liked him all right, but he made me feel young and self-conscious. He was sort of like a father—but a father I didn't know.

"The train was fine," I said. "I like trains."

He seemed to be waiting for me to say more.

"Trains make me feel—oh, I don't know—like something exciting is going to happen, like I'm on my way to adventure somewhere—"

I wasn't explaining myself very well, not really expressing the sense of anticipation that filled me as I watched scenery fly by a train window. On wintry days the land I traveled through was Iceland or the snowbound Arctic. Other times I was on the Orient Express, a spy escaping from some romantically dangerous European city. On a train I was never just Marjorie Loring from Sanderville, Indiana. But I couldn't really tell him that.

David mused a moment and then said, "Well, I think you might find Larrimore Hills a bit short on adventures and excitement."

I knew I was blushing, and I was grateful when Charlene interrupted us by saying, "Now don't bother Marjorie with a lot of questions."

Silver bracelets slid along her arm as she lifted

her hand and made a scolding gesture toward David.

"What we really want to know is if Marjorie wants to go out somewhere for fried chicken, or if we should go to that Italian place on Hawley Road and have lasagna and their marvelous garlic bread."

"You remember everything I like to eat," I said with such enthusiasm that I could see I had amused David.

"I'm not in the mood to cook tonight," Charlene said, as though on other nights she was.

David shifted himself into a standing position. "If we're going out for dinner, give me a few minutes to change."

After he had gone into the house, Charlene set down her glass of tea and said, "I think I'd better change too. Wherever we go, the air-conditioning will be too cool for this outfit. There are some magazines over there—" She motioned toward a table at the side of the patio. "I won't be long."

I could still smell her perfume after she had gone. I sat for a moment without even moving, thinking how great it was to be visiting Charlene and David. It was like a miracle. Mom and Dad were off to Italy for ten days with "The Group"—that's what Mom and Dad called them. The Group was a bunch of friends of theirs, married couples who played bridge together, went to the theater, and once a year took a trip somewhere. When the idea for the trip to Italy came up, I just assumed I'd stay with Trixie Donahue while Mom and Dad were gone. It was the only natural thing to do. Trixie was my best friend; she lived across the street from us; I knew her house as well as I knew my own, and she could say the same things.

But when I went over to talk to Trixie about staying with her, I found out she was planning to spend August on a camping trip with her parents.

"I didn't know you liked camping," I said. I felt abandoned. All my visions of goofing around at Trixie's for three weeks vanished—all-night TV in her room, the backyard barbecues her family loved, swapping clothes and jewelry, wearing all the eye shadow I wanted without Mom looking grieved. I had planned on having a ball at Trixie's, and she wouldn't even be home.

"I like camping okay," Trixie said. "I only went once before, when I was about ten."

I hadn't been her best friend then. So I didn't know anything about when she went camping.

"When did all this come up?" I wanted to know.

"Just yesterday," Trixie said. We were up in her room—where she had the TV I thought we'd watch all the late-late-late shows on, if I had stayed with her.

Maybe I looked disappointed—which I certainly was—because then Trixie said, "Hey, maybe you'd like to come along."

"Camping?" I wasn't sure her parents would want another kid along. They already had Trixie and her two younger brothers. Also, I wasn't sure I wanted to go camping. Was I the outdoor type? At picnics I was usually the one who walked into the poison ivy or got chased by a bee or sat down next to a snake.

But if I didn't go camping with Trixie, where would I stay? Grandma Loring's, probably. That wouldn't be very exciting. She was always nice to me, but she'd never want to drive to the shopping center or send out for pizza. The last time I stayed with her, she wanted to teach me to knit. And she was so far on the other side of town I'd *never* see Eddie Jackson—my secret love.

But I didn't have a chance to worry too much about any of that because when I went home to tell Mom that Trixie was going camping with her family, Mom had just received Charlene's invitation for me to visit her. While I was at Trixie Donahue's house, wondering if I should go on a camping trip, my cousin Charlene was on the phone, calling from Larrimore Hills.

"How did she know you were going to Italy?" I couldn't believe my luck.

"I just happened to write her a letter last week," Mom said. "And I mentioned that your dad and I were going to Italy in August. I wasn't hinting that you stay with her, but she says she'd be very happy to have you and she won't take no for an answer."

I certainly wouldn't say no! It was a miracle. And now there I was in Larrimore Hills.

When Charlene left the patio to change her pink silk outfit for something more suitable for an air-conditioned restaurant, I finally did go over to the table she had indicated. There were magazines, as she had said. But on top of the pile of magazines was a newpaper, with a headline too exciting to ignore.

INMATE ESCAPES ASYLUM

The subheadline read: "Terrorizes Surrounding Area."

It was just like a movie or TV plot. I forgot about the magazines and sat down in a chair by the table, holding the newspaper on my lap. I felt chills run along the skin of my arms as I read.

Saturday night an inmate at the Brightman Psychiatric Institution in downstate Illinois escaped despite security measures in effect at Brightman.

Residents of the small fishing community nearby have reported seeing a strange figure in the woods. The area is heavily wooded and sparsely populated. Residents are in fear for their lives.

I had a vision of a desolate, lonely landscape and a solitary house shrouded by the darkness of night. A maniacal face appears at the window of that house, revealed as a flash of lightning from a summer storm lights up the countryside.

I felt a chill of fear, imagining myself turning to the window in that house and seeing a crazed face peering in.

Then there would be a crash of glass as the windowpane was broken and the madman outside would lunge into the room. . . .

My cousin Charlene's luxurious home in Larrimore Hills was not the place to find a week-old newspaper on a patio table, but it didn't bother me at the time. I was too carried away by the newpaper story and by my own imagination. I was caught up in the terror of knowing an escaped lunatic was at large somewhere, even though it was hundreds of miles from me.

Chapter Two

WE WENT TO THE ITALIAN RESTAURANT for lasagna. David was rather quiet, but I decided that was his natural way. He did have an air of assurance about him, and I felt very sophisticated being escorted into the restaurant by him—and, of course, Charlene. Apparently they came to the restaurant frequently, because the hostess seemed to know them and chatted with Charlene as she led us toward a specially good table on a balcony area a few steps above the main room.

"Well, Marjorie," David said politely, "we're happy to have you visit us. I'm sorry that I have to leave on a business trip day after tomorrow, but I'm sure Charlene will find plenty of things to entertain you."

"No problem." Charlene tapped her fingers on

the gold cover of the menu lying beside her place. "Some of my friends are coming for lunch on Thursday," she said to us. "We have a lunch get-together once a month. It was my turn this week and I thought, 'Why cancel?' Anyway, they all want to meet you."

David arched an eyebrow and gave me a look that seemed to say he thought I might be less than thrilled to be with a houseful of chattering ladies. Well, four ladies, as it turned out. That probably would have seemed like a whole houseful to him when they got together talking and gossiping and admiring one another's clothes. But I was used to my mom's bridge club and the Sanderville Hospital Auxiliary meetings, and they weren't too bad. There were always terrific things to eat, and in the kitchen Trixie and I pigged out on salted nuts, lemon torte, and finger sandwiches decorated with olive slices.

"Then when David gets back from his business trip," Charlene continued, "we'll all go up to the lake for a few days. You'll love it there, Marjorie."

"I can hardly wait. Do you go there a lot in the summer?"

"No," Charlene said regretfully. "That's the only problem; we don't get there as often as we'd like. It's hard for David to get away from the office, so it's mostly weekends—" She was interrupted by a waiter asking if we were ready to order.

Shortly after we returned to the house, David

excused himself and went upstairs to bed. He had to be at his office early Monday morning. Charlene and I stayed up for a while and talked about old times back in Sanderville, when she was in high school and baby-sat me.

Finally we went up to bed too. It had been an exciting day: my last-minute packing at home that morning, the afternoon train trip, the excitement of being away from home.

I was still keyed-up when I got into bed, but I did fall asleep right away anyway.

The guest room at Charlene's house overlooked the patio and the garden behind the house. The next morning I stood by the window, brushing my hair and looking down, thinking how beautiful it was. Sunlight through the trees made a leafy pattern on the lawn, and I could see the sprinkler, pulled to the side, turned off, its silvery nozzle reflecting the light. A large tree in the center of the lawn was surrounded by a circle of large red flowers I didn't know. But I recognized petunias growing beside the hedges that bordered the south and west sides of the garden.

Beyond the tall lilac bushes I could see a neighboring garden where a woman in a huge straw hat was reading in a lawn chair.

In some other yard I couldn't see, a dog was barking. He stopped after a moment and everything was peaceful again.

David had left for the office long before I went downstairs that Monday morning. Worn out from excitement, I had slept late. Charlene was on the patio, which at that hour of the day was cool and shady, a perfect place to sit and have breakfast, looking out at the dappled morning light in the garden.

Apparently the morning mail had already come. A small pile of envelopes and a new *Town And Country* magazine lay on the table.

Charlene had eaten breakfast, and she sat with her chair pushed slightly away from the table. The hem of the long, flowery lounging robe she was wearing trailed down on the patio bricks. She was reading a letter, and when I came out of the house she looked at me as though her mind were a million miles away.

"I've just received the strangest letter," she said. "It came in the morning mail." Her voice sort of drifted off, and she looked down at the letter with a puzzled expression.

I sat down at the table and said, "What's strange about it?"

She hesitated a moment and then shrugged, as if she were thinking to herself that there was no harm in letting me see it. She handed me the letter, which was not very long. It was really just one sentence.

"Ask your husband if the accident at Greenwood Lake was really an accident."

There was no date, no signature, just those cryptic words. "Ask your husband if the accident at Greenwood Lake was really an accident."

"Isn't that weird?" Charlene asked and waited for my reaction.

To me the letter was more confusing than weird.

"What accident? What's Greenwood Lake?"

"Greenwood Lake is a resort up in northern Wisconsin." Charlene fingered a string of white beads she was wearing. "It was where David's first wife drowned. I guess you probably didn't know about that."

I shook my head. "No, I didn't. I just knew he was a widower."

"Well, his wife drowned. And when we started dating he told me about it. And it definitely *was* an accident. I can't imagine who would write something like this."

She took the letter from me and studied it again, shaking her head at the mystery of it. "Who would write such a thing? It's preposterous to suggest that David had anything to do with his wife's death."

At that I was too startled to say anything. I couldn't imagine quiet, dignified David Kensington having anything to do with drowning anyone. Or so I told myself.

Even so, I wanted to hear all the details.

"How did the accident happen?"

Charlene didn't answer at once. Then she said, "They had rented a cottage for a few weeks at Greenwood Lake. Apparently one morning his wife—Rosemary was her name—swam out to a diving raft that was anchored offshore. They both loved to swim and swam out to it often."

I forgot then that I hadn't had my breakfast yet and that I had been starving when I came downstairs. I forgot about everything except listening to my cousin Charlene. I could picture a raft rocking gently on small swells of blue-green waves. I could see David and Rosemary climbing up on the raft, glistening wet from their swim from shore . . . Rosemary shaking back wet hair. I could see them stretching themselves to sun on the gently rocking raft . . . then practicing dives . . . later, swimming back to shore and walking up a sandy, grassy slope to a cottage on the shoreline.

"They think Rosemary swam out to the raft. And whether she tried to swim back again without resting no one knows for sure. But that's what they thought had happened. She just didn't make it back."

We sat in silence for a few moments after Charlene told me that. To drown seemed like a specially horrible death to me. They say your lungs feel as if they're bursting, and I know that's true. One time in a school swim class I tried to rescue a girl who was having trouble. I saw her floundering and just rushed right over. Everything I'd heard about rescuing drowning people went right out of my head. "They try to pull you under. Don't do it unless you have lifeguard training." Etcetera, etcetera—right out of my head.

There were long poles lying beside the pool for

rescuing people. We were told never to try to jump in and do it personally. I forgot all that. I grabbed her, a skinny girl named Marcia something-or-other. I wouldn't have thought she had so much strength. She seized me with hysterical relief, pushing me down below her and keeping me down as she tried to climb on my shoulders. I was her buoy to the surface. I knew I was going to die. The more I struggled to get away, the more fiercely poor Marcia held me down under the water.

An eternity passed. If there was any commotion around the pool, it was in a world removed from mine. For me nothing existed but Marcia's feet and legs thrashing above my head, the terror of the water heavy around me, and the certain sense that I was going to die.

At last someone on the deck held out a rescue pole to Marcia. She grabbed it and let go of me. Nothing had ever looked so wonderful to me as the green walls of the pool area when I finally came up for air.

Someone pushed a pole toward me too, and helping hands came to pull me out of the water when I got to the side of the pool. I was surrounded by girls. Trixie was at my side instantly, and as I stood gasping to get my breath a frightened swim teacher said, "Marjorie! How many times have you been told not to try to rescue someone yourself? We have *poles*."

"Drowning is such an awful way to die," I said to Charlene with a little shudder.

Now that she had told me about David's wife, the letter made more sense. Still, it was a queet sort of scary letter.

"But who wrote the letter? Why didn't they sign it?" I felt frustrated. It wasn't fair not to know.

"It had to be anonymous," Charlene said thoughtfully. "No one would want to be responsible for such a dreadful accusation against David, even if it is totally ridiculous. It's probably somebody's idea of a prank—like those phone calls kids make. You know, just pick a number at random in the phone book and say, 'I saw what you did,' or something like that. It gets the people all worried. Everybody's done something they want to hide."

"Did you used to do that?" I asked. "Call strange people on the phone and say, 'I saw what you did.' "

"Sure, when I was a kid." Charlene smiled and smoothed her golden hair with an angelic gesture. "But the most fun wasn't strangers, it was calling up people I really knew, saying things like 'Where is your husband tonight? Is he *really* working late?' That really rattled Mrs. Phillips, the lady who lived next door to us. She knew her husband fooled around, but she always hoped he'd reform. He never did, not him.

"And then there were the two little old ladies who lived across the street. I used to call them up and say, 'There's someone outside your house, hiding in the bushes.' It gave them a good scare."

It didn't seem like a very nice thing to do, even just for fun. Before I could think out the rest of that thought and try to connect the angelic-looking Charlene with those pranks, she closed her eyes and sighed. "That was light-years ago. This letter is here and now."

Her eyes opened slowly as she said, "And the best place for it is in the wastepaper basket."

She tore the letter into small pieces and let the pieces flutter down into an empty plate on the table.

"Are you going to tell David?" I thought I would feel awkward when David came home that evening, knowing somebody had written such a strange letter about him.

"Oh, *no*." Charlene sounded shocked that I could even think of discussing the letter with David. "It's too silly to bother him with. Besides, it would make him sad to remember the accident." She paused a moment and then she added, "We won't mention it at all, to *anyone*. Okay?"

"Okay," I said.

I felt my appetite returning after we had decided the letter was a prank. The tiny torn scraps lying in the plate didn't seem as menacing as the whole letter had seemed.

"Are you hungry?" Charlene asked.

"Starved!"

"Good. I have some marvelous strawberries— and I make a very good omelet." Charlene got up with a swish of her flowery robe and started toward the kitchen. "I'll have some more coffee and keep you company while you eat."

I thought I would forget all about the letter, but it came back to me off and on during the day.

Not with any great force or premonition of things to come, nothing like that.

It was just sort of there in the back of my mind. A vision of a raft rocking on the water was superimposed with the single sentence of the letter, like a double exposure on a snapshot.

Chapter Three

OUR PLAN FOR THAT FIRST AFTERNOON was to shop. Charlene said I *had* to see the Larrimore Hills shopping center. She said shopping centers were the delight of every woman's life.

I could certainly go along with that. Trixie Donahue and I spent a lot of our time and just about all of our money at the shopping center in Sanderville. We trudged tirelessly from store to store, plotting purchases, looking for sales, keeping an eye out for boys we liked, who unfortunately didn't haunt the shopping center as frequently as Trixie and I did.

The Larrimore Hills shops were in an enclosed mall. There was a spacious central atrium with a fountain and streams of water spurting from stone pitchers on the shoulders of stone mermaids.

The sound of that water was a pervasive underlying rhythm throughout the mall.

It was a more luxurious shopping mall than Sanderville's—by a long way. All the shoppers looked rich. Even the little kids looked rich. Charlene swept in and out of all the expensive boutiques as casually as Trixie and I checked out two dollar and ninety-nine cent earrings at the bargain counters in Sanderville.

Trixie and I were both about the same size, short and—well, not what you'd call skinny. We both wanted to lose weight and grow taller—and maybe somehow turn into glamorous redheads or blondes. But we were still only about five feet tall, and likely to remain brown haired and brown eyed. Trixie did threaten to dye her hair someday, and then she would be blond at last.

Charlene was everything *I* wanted to be: five feet five, slender, blond, beautiful. She could look sophisticated when she wanted to, or she could put on a pair of jeans, tie her hair up in a ponytail with a bright scarf, and look sixteen. She was tan—*of course*—and her hair was even lighter in the summer than in the other seasons. She wore a lot of deep pink, which looked great with her tan skin and sun-bleached hair.

I felt small and plump and blissfully happy trailing along beside her through the exclusive shops of the Larrimore Hills mall.

We had a stylishly late lunch about two-thirty at a restaurant in the mall named Pierre's. It was decorated like a French country inn with whitewashed brick walls and gleaming dark oak floors and ceiling beams. There was a vase of yellow daisies on each table, and the food was mostly things like quiche and crepes, which I rarely ate. Usually where Trixie and I went it was hamburgers or pizza.

Charlene had just bought some new shorts to wear at the lake, pink sandals, and a matching beach bag, so we were rustling with packages as we arranged ourselves at our table. I saw the way the waiter looked at Charlene, and I thought we would get good service.

When he left with our order, she leaned across the table toward me and said, "That waiter thinks you're cute."

"Me? Oh, he wouldn't notice *me*."

"Why not?" Charlene settled back into her chair. "You're a very pretty girl. You must have lots of boyfriends back in Sanderville."

"Oh, not so many." I shifted self-consciously and looked up at the French country inn beams.

"Come on now," Charlene said teasingly. "Tell me about your boyfriends."

So I told her about Eddie Jackson, a boy at Sanderville High who, alas, barely knew I was alive.

"Trixie and I both have crushes on him," I admitted hopelessly. "Trixie is my best friend."

Charlene nodded and smoothed her hair.

"And lots of other girls at school do too—have crushes on Eddie, that is."

Talking about Eddie Jackson made him seem suddenly close. Wouldn't it be wonderful if he came walking into Pierre's that very moment and saw me sitting with Charlene at the table with yellow daisies.

"Hi," I'd say casually, and he'd pull up an extra chair and sit at our table for a while. He had done that one time at the Pizza Hut in Sanderville. There were about six kids at the table, so I couldn't say it was because I was at the table that he sat down. Though I certainly wish it was.

Our waiter brought quiche florentine and coffee in a delicate white china pot for Charlene.

"Eddie's captain of the basketball team." I made that sound pretty important.

I wanted to tell Charlene all about Eddie. How he cruised around in a red Camaro. I suppose it was his father's or mother's. But maybe it was his own. I had never ridden in it, of course, so I had no occasion to ask him whose it was.

"He sounds darling," Charlene said.

She was trying to be a good sport, showing an interest in Eddie and all my chatter. I knew Eddie Jackson was of no importance to her really. As I watched her stir cream into her coffee, I had a feeling that she was thinking about the letter, that the memory of it was still lingering in her mind, as it was in mine. But neither of us wanted to say so.

Chapter Four

WE CAME HOME FROM THE MALL WITH our arms full. Besides carrying some of the things Charlene had bought, I had a new record for myself and a pair of red earrings for Trixie—souvenirs of my trip. I knew Trixie would love the earrings, and I could hardly wait to give them to her.

We also brought dinner home in little white paper cartons from a Chinese take-out place: egg rolls, shrimp chop suey, rice, and sweet and sour pork.

We came home in the late afternoon—almost evening.

"Home at last," Charlene said, dropping her packages on the blue velvet bench in the foyer. She looked as fresh and energetic as she had looked before we set out. "Put your record on, and we'll get dinner organized."

To the strains of my new record we set the dining-room table and put the Chinese food in pans to warm on the stove.

"Is David always this late?" I asked. It was nearly seven. Sunlight was fading in the garden. The silence of evening settled around the house. It was so much more quiet than Sanderville, as though money had cushioned all the noise and distractions of life. The houses were on larger lots and were at a greater distance from one another, each cocooned in a velvety green lawn and remote gentility. There were no sounds of shouting children, lawn mowers, noisy cars going by in the street.

"No, he's not usually this late," Charlene remarked cheerfully. She broke off a piece of dinner roll—warm from the oven—and handed me the other half. "So you won't starve," she said.

A moment later she said, "Oh, here he comes now," and we could see the flash of late-day sunlight on the chrome of David's car as it was driven into the driveway.

"He probably stayed late at the office tonight because he's going to be off on that business trip tomorrow. There're always last-minute things to take care of."

I stood by the dining-room window and watched David walking from the driveway along the flag-stone path toward the house. I wondered what he would think if he knew someone had hinted that he had drowned his wife.

He was carrying a briefcase, loosening his tie as he walked. He's happy to be home, I thought—but things are not always what they seem.

I felt guilty during dinner. Every time I looked at David, I thought about the letter and the raft on Greenwood Lake.

David ate with the same deliberate manner that I imagined he would conduct a business meeting or arrange lunch with a client. With the touch of gray at his temples and his distinguished, intellectual look, I could easily picture him teaching philosophy or medieval literature at a university, wearing leather elbow patches on a tweed jacket, smoking a pipe, strolling across campus for a conference with the dean.

In reality, he was an investments counselor for a large firm in Chicago, a firm with branch offices and clients throughout the Midwest, so he often traveled. I felt a sense of relief to think that he was leaving in the morning on one of these business trips.

After dinner we sat on the patio. Charlene and David had coffee and I had a dish of ice cream. Well, who could diet on a vacation!

The conversation got around to my mom and dad's trip, and David seemed really interested. "I was in Italy once," he said, reserved, but with more enthusiasm than he had shown since I arrived. "Where are your parents now?"

"Let me think—" I had the itinerary of their tour in my suitcase upstairs, but I didn't have it committed to memory.

"Get the tour information and we'll track them down," Charlene said, waving me upstairs with a laugh and a gesture.

I ran through a house growing dusky with summer twilight. In the living room one last stray fleck of light fell on a crystal bowl, and in a shadowed corner a grandfather clock struck the hour with an enchanting rhythm that I didn't take time to stop and listen to.

My own room was enchanted, too, at that moment between light and darkness. A hazy glow flooded in from the windows, deep blue, dusky, like a mist seeping across everything. Nothing had a solid, hard edge. The bed, chair, dresser, tables, all were undefined, melting into the dark of evening. The dresser mirror shimmered with shadows and mystery.

My suitcase was by the windows, and before I knelt to open it and find the tour itinerary, I glanced through the window down to the patio and garden.

What a different place the garden was from the morning one of dappled sunlight. A gauzy shroud of gray had floated across the sparkling green of daytime; the red flowers planted around the central tree were dark stalks blending into the great stalk of the tree; the petunias were faint white ghosts clustered at the garden's edge.

It was like looking into a place I had never seen before.

On the patio, too, dusk had fallen. I could see David and Charlene sitting at the patio table—the same table where Charlene had sat reading her strange letter only that morning.

David and Charlene were as lost in twilight as the garden. And then suddenly Charlene leaned forward and lighted a candle on the table. I saw her face for a moment in the candlelight as she smiled at David. He didn't reach out to take her hand in his, or kiss her, which would have been romantic there in the dark garden. He sat very still and straight in his chair, and after a moment Charlene turned her head away. I saw the swing of her silky yellow hair, lighted by candlelight.

"They're still in Rome."

I hung over the travel brochure in the trembling light of the candle on the patio table, and then passed the brochure to Charlene.

Assisi, Perugia, Venice, Genoa, still lay ahead. But that day, that moment, Mom and Dad and The Group were still in Rome. Their flight had landed there that morning and they had two days of sight-seeing in Rome before going on.

"Ah, Rome," David said with an air of fond reminiscence. "They'll see the Colosseum and the Spanish Steps, the Villa Borghese."

"The Trevi Fountain," Charlene added. "Did you

know, Marjorie, that if you toss a coin in the Trevi Fountain you will return to Rome someday? Isn't that romantic."

It *was* romantic. I thought of Eddie Jackson. I thought of being with him and tossing coins into the Trevi Fountain. He would be holding my hand and looking at me instead of the fountain.

I wondered what he was doing now, miles away in Sanderville, on a hot summer night in August.

And right then, I had a sense of longing for Sanderville. A real longing that came over me quite unexpectedly. Things were somehow more *real* there, more down-to-earth. I thought of the lavish fountain splashing water in gushing sprays at the Larrimore Hills mall, and for a moment I just wanted to be with Trixie and hear her say, "Let's go to McDonalds" or, "Let's check out the jeans at The Gap."

Sanderville and home, Trixie and Eddie, were a long way away that night. They seemed as far away as Rome, Italy, and Mom and Dad.

Loneliness washed over me and I thought with disgust, Can I be homesick at almost sixteen, almost sixteen?

I was uprooted from both Sanderville, Indiana, and Rome, Italy, and whisked to China as Charlene opened a little paper package from our carry-out Chinese dinner.

"Fortune cookies," she announced, spreading the cookies across the patio table.

There were three.

We read them in the flickering candlelight. By then the garden was dark. In the house only a small light left on over the kitchen stove was visible.

"You first," Charlene said, taking a cookie from the table and pressing it into my hand.

I cracked open the cookie and pulled out the thin strip of paper. " 'Things are not always what they seem.' "

"A good thing to remember," David said. I was disappointed. I wanted, "You will be rich and travel all over the world," or something like that.

"You're next," Charlene told David, and his long, thin fingers pried apart the crisp sides of the fortune cookie.

" 'The wise man knows life is a mystery never solved.' "

I looked at David's face in the candlelight. It was shadowed and unfamiliar, a stranger's face. "Are these all 'advice' cookies?" he asked. "Isn't anybody getting a 'fortune'?"

"I will, I will," Charlene promised lightly. She crumbled her cookie and drew out the slip of paper inside.

" 'To each is given the reward he deserves.' "

Was that a "fortune" or only more wise advice? While I was trying to figure it out, Charlene said, "I already have everything I want." She was smiling tenderly at David. "I don't need any rewards."

Chapter Five

I WONDERED IF THERE WOULD BE A SECOND letter that next morning.

David had left on his business trip before the mail delivery. And although Charlene appeared nonchalant as she glanced through the mail, I knew she had to be wondering if there would be another mysterious, unsigned letter.

That's certainly what I was wondering.

I watched Charlene shift through the assortment of envelopes, and I tried to see whether any envelope looked as if it might have an anonymous letter inside.

At that time I was more curious than scared.

Being scared would come later.

"No 'letter' today?" I couldn't resist asking. I tried to sound amused, to show Charlene I really knew the letter the day before had been a joke—however poor.

She shook her head disparagingly and made a face. "Wasn't that the most outrageous thing? Honestly!" She tossed aside the envelopes as though she had no further interest in the mail now that she had assured herself there was no second letter.

Still, I had a feeling that if someone were having fun sending weird letters to people we might get another one.

That was Tuesday.

There was no letter on Wednesday either.

I began to think less about the whole thing. I had probably been dramatizing it in my own mind. Besides, Charlene and I were busy having fun.

On Tuesday we drove a long way out into the country to find a rustic antique shop and dining room Charlene had heard about. We got lost twice—my fault, as I was the map reader. But we finally found the place. Charlene bought a beautiful old hand-carved jewelry box and a large, tarnished brass dog doorstop, which she intended to polish and put in front of the fireplace in her living room. We came home after dark, tired but exhilarated with the adventures of the day.

On Wednesday we did some shopping for the luncheon Charlene was going to have for her friends on Thursday.

We went to a small gourmet shop to buy a certain tea Charlene wanted. At an exclusive bakery—decorated with brass rails, white tiles, and hanging plants—we bought two loaves of crusty french bread and a dozen pecan tarts.

Charlene's shopping expeditions apparently did not include crowded supermarkets with fussy kids being pushed in shopping carts, people returning bottles for refunds, or long lines at checkout counters. Charlene's shopping was a lot more elegant—and a lot more expensive.

That Wednesday afternoon when the grocery shopping was done, we carried the brass dog outside to be polished.

The weather, which had been so perfect the past days, turned muggy that afternoon. Leaves hung motionless from the branches of the trees that shaded the patio. The sky was pale and dull, the color sadness would be if sadness had a color.

Charlene polished the brass dog with the total absorption of a happy child with a new toy. There seemed to be nothing else on her mind.

"You'll wear him away," I said, kneeling beside her on the grassy lawn of the garden, where the brass dog looked out of place and not quite so large as he had looked when he was in the house. Around us on the grass were scraps of polishing cloths, damp with brass polish and dark with tarnish.

The dog glistened even in the somber light of the overcast sky.

When Charlene was satisfied at last, we carried the dog indoors and put him in his place of honor as guard of the fireplace.

He seemed at home there, with the blue silk sofa

and chairs, the pendulum of the great grandfather clock in the corner swinging its changeless rhythm, glossy magazines spread on the long, marble-topped cocktail table: *Architectural Digest, Vogue, Smithsonian.*

I thought it must be an even more lovely room in wintertime, with a fire in the fireplace and snow falling past the panes of the french doors that led to the side garden.

It was the most beautiful house I had ever seen. The brass dog was lucky to have such a splendid room to live in and a mistress as sweet and beautiful as my cousin Charlene.

On Thursday morning, when I had almost stopped expecting another letter—the second one arrived.

It was not quite so brief as the first, and not nearly so easy to dismiss as a mean, harmless joke.

The accident at Greenwood Lake was not an accident. Your husband murdered his first wife, and he is going to murder you.

He has already tried—and he will try again.

Chapter Six

CHARLENE'S HAND WAS SHAKING A BIT AS she reached out to take back the letter she had given me to read.

What the letter said had astonished me so completely I couldn't think of anything to say.

"This is going too far," Charlene said nervously. Then she said, "Goodness, Marjorie, don't look like that. It—it can't be *true*."

Silently she read the letter through again and bit her lower lip to stop its trembling.

"Do you think there *could* be anything—I mean any truth—about the accident not being an accident?" I asked cautiously. I was beginning to feel frightened. I hardly knew David Kensington or what kind of a man he was. Maybe Charlene didn't know him as well as she thought she did. My mind was racing. Wasn't it always the quiet, nonsuspicious types who were guilty of crimes? It was that way a lot of times in movies and TV shows and books. Maybe David was a compulsive wife-murderer. I thought if I turned and saw him unexpectedly standing behind me at the edge of the patio, I would scream.

I wished Charlene would scold me for even suggesting anything bad about David. But she didn't. She was hypnotized by the letter, and when she looked up at last her eyes were troubled, her face pale beneath the tan.

"This is nonsense—that's all it is." She made an effort to keep her voice steady. With an almost violent motion—as though determined to stop the direction of her own thoughts—she crushed the letter into a ball and held it in her clenched fist.

"Don't you have *any* idea who might be writing these letters? If you just think hard, maybe you'll think of somebody."

I wanted *so much* for Charlene to think of someone.

She gestured impatiently. "Heavens, Marjorie, *lots* of people know about Rosemary drowning. Occasionally we still see friends of David's who knew him when he was married to Rosemary—"

"Maybe one of them hates you and wants to make trouble," I said, interrupting her. I was grabbing ideas out of the hot, sultry morning air. "Maybe it's some woman who wants to have David for herself."

Charlene put her elbows on the table. Still clutching the letter in one hand, she pressed the other to her forehead. "I'm getting a headache. It's just all nonsense. David wouldn't want to hurt me—" But she sounded unsure and fearful.

"Was that drowning investigated?" I frowned suspiciously. "I mean *really* investigated?"

Charlene nodded, eyes closed, hand pressed to her forehead.

"Well, why doesn't this person, whoever wrote the letter, go to the police if he thinks it wasn't an accident?"

"It *was* an accident—this, this *person,* is just crazy." I felt she was trying to persuade herself more than me.

"Maybe he's got proof, somehow. . . ." I was still grasping at straws.

Charlene shook her head wearily. "It's been four years. What kind of proof of anything like that turns up after four years?"

"It could," I insisted stubbornly. "Maybe they just didn't investigate carefully enough at the time."

Charlene moved her hand from her forehead. She stared bleakly across the garden. "David said they investigated it thoroughly enough for what it was, a simple case of drowning. There was absolutely no doubt that Rosemary drowned right there that morning in Greenwood Lake. No mystery about it. No one killed her someplace else and dumped her body in the lake—nothing like that. Lake water was in her lungs. There wasn't a mark on her body."

I sat silently for a moment, wanting to believe what she said. But it left so many unanswered questions—like who wrote those letters, was David really a murderer, and if he was, how the letter writer had discovered it.

Charlene was a little calmer now. She loosened her grip on the crumpled letter and seemed almost to forget she was still holding it.

"It was a terrible experience for David. He said Rosemary was always the first one up and was usually reading on the porch or sunning herself on the raft. That morning he couldn't find her. He couldn't imagine where she had gone so early.

"He walked over to the lodge, on the off chance she had gone there. No one at the lodge had seen her. Nor had anyone in the other cottages around the lodge.

"By noon he was frantic. But it wasn't until much later that they actually found Rosemary's body. Then they established the time of death as early that morning."

Charlene's voice faded. "It was a terrible thing for him. . . ."

For Rosemary mainly, I thought. I wasn't sure I felt sorry for David.

"David told me he testified at the inquest that Rosemary wasn't a good enough swimmer to swim out to the raft and back in one spurt. He could do it, but not Rosemary. He said he thought maybe she was trying to see if she could do it, maybe to surprise him. Whatever the reason, it was the verdict at the inquest that Rosemary had overextended herself."

We sat in uneasy thought for a few moments, and then I said, "What about that part about killing you? 'He has already tried—and he will try again.' What does that mean?"

Charlene spread her hands in a dramatic gesture of surrender. "How should I know what that means! It's crazy, all of it."

"You can't think of any time David tried to kill you?"

Even as I said the words, I knew it was a strange thing to be asking someone.

"No."

Charlene gave me an icy stare, and I felt like a complete idiot.

"No," she elaborated, mimicking me. "I can't think of any time David tried to kill me. Does this look like a home where people are trying to kill each other?"

I lowered my eyes, wallowing in embarrassment. Mom says I always rattle on when I should be quiet. She's right, I guess. It had been a stupid thing to ask Charlene.

Around us the garden lay in the colorless light of a dull, muggy summer day. Surely it had to rain soon. All day the day before I had thought it would rain at any moment. It never had. There had only been the oppressive, heavy, humid air, the tension of rain to come.

I was aware of a touch on my arm. Charlene had reached across the table. Her fingers felt cool as she patted my arm. "Don't pay any attention to me. I just don't like anonymous letters"—a light laugh, as if anyone would—"and I took it out on you."

"That's okay."

I looked up gratefully, and she gave my arm another quick pat. "Enough of this ridiculous murder talk," she said firmly. "We don't want to spoil your visit."

She hesitated as though something had just occurred to her.

"And we don't want to spoil your parents' trip with something that's nothing. If they call, don't say anything about these letters. Let them have the good time they deserve."

I didn't think it likely that my mom and dad would call me all the way from Italy, but, of course, anything was possible.

"I won't say anything," I promised. Everything Charlene had said made sense, and I certainly didn't want to be the one to upset Mom and Dad on their long-anticipated dream trip in Italy. Especially over something that was probably nothing.

"I need some fresh coffee," Charlene said, determined to be cheerful. I stared out over the garden and listened to her footsteps on the brick of the patio floor, the sound of the screen door closing behind her as she went into the kitchen.

When she came back out to the patio a few minutes later, she didn't have the letter with her. I wondered if she had thrown it away like the first one.

"It sure looks like rain," she said, sitting down opposite me at the patio table. "Well, let it. It won't spoil our plans."

I had forgotten all about the four ladies coming for lunch.

"By the way," she added, "here's a letter for you."

I had a funny feeling when she said that. Who was writing to me? Was I going to get a mysterious letter too? As Charlene handed me the bright orange envelope with a rainbow arching over my name—nothing at all like the inexpensive plain white envelopes Charlene's letters arrived in—I was greatly relieved to see Trixie's name in the upper left-hand corner.

"It's from Trixie. She's my best friend, remember?"

Charlene nodded, not looking up as she poured coffee.

"She's camping with her family."

After the awful letter about David, Trixie's bright orange and rainbowed envelope seemed like something from another, brighter world.

I pulled the single sheet of orange paper from the envelope and laid it on the table.

"Dear Marjorie," I began to read aloud.

"How is everything? What are you doing? We're at a camping area in Fitz-allen Woods. It's really neat. So far nobody has walked into any poison ivy or anything like that. Ha-ha. Bobby and I will hike into town so I can mail this to you. We're going on to White Wood next week, and stay for four or five days. That's where the good fishing is, and that's what my dad wants. See you when you get back. Can you believe summer vacation is already more than half over?"

No, I couldn't believe that summer vacation was already more than half over. I folded the letter and slid it back into its envelope.

"You'll have to write and tell her what you've been doing," Charlene said.

"I can't write to her while she's out in the woods camping."

"Of course not. I wasn't thinking." Charlene lowered her eyes guiltily, so I could see she had been thinking about her own letter all the time and hardly listening to mine.

I felt kind of cut off from everybody: Mom and Dad in Italy—in Genoa that day; I had checked the itinerary that morning—Trixie at a campsite in a woods I had never heard of, a place where I couldn't reach her if I did write a letter.

Rain began to fall while we were clearing the breakfast things. Sheltered in the doorway, I stood watching the rain for a few moments, feeling lonesome for Trixie, and worried about the letters to Charlene. My mind seemed full of so many thoughts as I watched the rain. It was not a violent thunder-and-lightning rain, only a silent downpouring from a dreary summer sky. The rain, falling straight and dark through the hot, still, summer morning, brought with it a sadness, a melancholy that mingled with a sort of dropping-off feeling in the pit of my stomach as I thought of how much I still had to learn about the adult world.

I thought of the yard at home and how, if it rained hard, white blossoms from the spirea bushes got beaten off and lay like snow across the summer grass.

Chapter Seven

WE WENT INTO THE HOUSE, PUT THE breakfast dishes in the dishwasher, and began preparations for the luncheon.

I helped Charlene make hors d'oeuvres, brought out silver dishes for nuts and candy, and put two tall white candles in beautiful crystal candlesticks. There was a quality of unreality about all these routine preparations. The windows streamed with rain and the house was so eerily silent that our voices and the clatter of dishes and silverware couldn't dispel the quiet.

When everything was done, and I was dressed and ready, I wandered into the living room. I stood by the french doors and watched the rain streaking the panes. It had not let up all morning. It was probably going to be an all-day rain. Already the grass looked squishy and sodden. Puddles were forming in the crevices between the flagstones in the garden. I put my finger against the glass of the door and trailed it along in the wake of a rivulet making a zigzag course down the pane. At one point it went sideways for a few inches before it started downward again. All around me the room was silent, washed by the dull light of the rainy day, and scented with water like an undersea castle. The brass dog sat motionless on the hearth by the fireplace. The ticking of the clock was finally muted by the steady drip of rain falling in the garden.

Ten minutes later the living room was resounding with voices and laughter as the guests arrived almost simultaneously and burst in with a flurry of bright summer dresses and dripping umbrellas. They hugged Charlene, complaining about the weather.

"Hello! Hello!" Charlene put her cheek to each guest's cheek and made a quick puckered kiss into the air.

"And this is your cousin Marjorie!" the ladies said. I was the center of undivided attention—a small, dark-haired girl in a white lacy dress whose reliable world had begun to seem another place entirely; as though, like Alice, I had stepped through into a dangerous wonderland. What would the women have said if I told them that only a few hours before Charlene and I had been talking about whether or not David was a murderer.

Instead, I said all the right things, nodding and smiling as each guest was introduced.

"I'll only give you first names," Charlene said, putting her arm across my shoulders affectionately as she began the introductions. "First names are all you really need to know. This is Dottie—this is Madge—this is Eleanor—and this is Loretta."

I knew I'd never keep them all straight. They were all Charlene's age, or older, and very much alike: beautifully dressed, with expensively cut hair, golf-course tans, and real jewelry. And sometimes they all seemed to talk at once.

Gradually they got settled in the living room, and as Charlene and I served the hors d'oeuvres the new brass dog took my place as a center of attention. For which I was certainly grateful. Everybody staring at me and talking about how cute I was was embarrassing. The ladies loved the dog. They all loved antiques, or at least liked to say they did. Charlene told them where she had bought the dog and they all said, "oh," they must go there sometime. The tall one—Madge, I think—burrowed down into her purse and came up with a shiny gold pen and said, "wait," she must write down the directions to where this marvelous place was. After that the conversation plunged abruptly into some bit of Larrimore Hills gossip revolving around the new golf links at the country club being not so good as had been hoped despite all the money spent by you-know-who. Heads nodded in agreement with this. Bracelets slid along tan arms; fingers fiddled with strands of beads; voices rose and fell and overlapped.

I passed more hors d'oeuvres, and every once in a while I overheard someone say to Charlene, "Your cousin Marjorie is so cute."

One lady asked me a few questions about Sanderville. She had never heard of Sanderville, so naturally she was curious.

Another lady didn't want any hors d'oeuvres because she was on a diet.

"Don't tempt me, sweetheart," she said, waving me away.

She was already thin, but I guess she wanted to be thinner. I wondered what she would eat for lunch. While the other guests ate hors d'oeuvres she admired her fingernails, which looked quite freshly done and were very long and glamorous and worthy of admiration. I certainly admired them.

Although Miss Fingernails only nibbled at lunch, the other women loved everything Charlene and I had fixed. They sat at the table laughing and talking with such obvious enjoyment that I forgot for a while that it was raining outside. Even so, there was an undercurrent to the gaiety of the luncheon. I felt it in the pauses between laughter. Like something was closing in.

The rain fell without a letup the whole afternoon.

I thought I was the only one who could see that Charlene was distracted, as if something else were on her mind. But as we were leaving the dining room after lunch, I heard one of her friends ask, "Char, is there something wrong? You look worried."

She said this aside to Charlene as we were leaving the dining room, and I wasn't close enough to hear Charlene's murmured reply. Would she tell her friend about the letters? I didn't think so. She had told me she wanted the letters to be just between the two of us.

At the same time that I was straining, unsuccessfully, to hear Charlene's answer, one of the ladies asked me, "When is David coming back?"

We stood in the living-room doorway.

"In about ten days," I said. "Then we're all going up to the cottage in Michigan."

"Ten days?" The woman who had asked about David looked surprised. "I didn't think his business trips were ever that long."

"Yes, sometimes they are," Charlene said casually, coming up behind us just then. "Not usually, but sometimes. He's driving this time, and that adds time."

"You must miss him," the lady with the long fingernails said coyly. "Such a handsome man."

Charlene said, "Yes, of course, I miss him very much."

I looked more closely at Miss Fingernails, a pretty brunette wearing a lavender dress and gold jewelry, and I wondered if she had her eye on David and was trying to make trouble by writing accusing letters.

It was the most foolish of all my ideas about who might have written the letters.

It was only that I wanted so very much to know who had written the letters, and why. The idea that it might be one of the four women sitting in the living room at that very moment appealed to my sense of drama.

But of course it wasn't one of them at all.

When the ladies left about four o'clock, the afternoon was coming to an early end because of the dark skies and the rain.

We had served tea in the living room after lunch, and Charlene brought an empty tray from the kitchen and went around the living room collecting the teacups. Suddenly she set the tray on a table by the sofa as though it was no longer important.

"I've just remembered something, Marjorie. Something that happened a couple of weeks ago." She sat down on the edge of the sofa cushion and looked at me with a peculiar expression.

Instinctively I knew that what she was saying had something to do with the mysterious letters. It was as if we were continuing our morning conversation without the interruption of the afternoon.

"You remember what the letter said about David trying to kill me?"

Remember? I had the whole letter memorized. And that sentence stood out. "He has already tried—and he will try again."

I sat down on a chair by the sofa and pressed my

hands together. They felt prickly and shaky. My legs felt shaky, too, so it was good to sit down.

"Charlene—" I started, my voice hushed with fright. "Did he really try to kill you once?"

I thought maybe we ought to get up and get out of the house to some safe place. It was an overreaction, as David was hundreds of miles away and we were as safe in the house as we would have been anywhere. Except maybe a police station. I thought I would feel very safe at a police station. But could we go to the police station with only anonymous letters and scary feelings?

"It was a couple of weeks ago—I'd forgotten all about it until just now," Charlene said slowly. "David and I had tickets to a program at the Chicago Civic Theater for a Friday evening. I thought I'd take an early-afternoon train and get a little shopping done before I met David for dinner and the program. We had it all arranged. Then suddenly, that very morning, he decided to take the train instead of driving into the city. He never does that, so I was surprised. He said he had some business to look over and had no other time to do it.

"So *I* was to drive in, so we'd have the car later. I didn't mind—it just seemed odd that he hadn't said anything until the last minute.

"Anyway, I left here about two o'clock. I figured I'd be in the city and parked by a little after three, and still have a couple of hours to shop. I had just gotten onto the expressway, and I was going pretty fast—over the limit—but I usually do and David

knows that. All of a sudden one of the tires blew out
and I skidded across two lanes and ended up on the
shoulder. I could have been killed.''

I felt all tingly and shivery again.

"You mean you think David did something to the
tire of the car, and then made up a story about
having to take the train so you would be in an
accident!"

I was horrified. Could someone do something to a
tire that would cause a blow-out, not right away, not
while Charlene was on the quiet streets of Larrimore Hills, but later when she was racing along the
expressway? Speedways, my dad calls them.

"I was just lucky," Charlene said. "Everybody
said so. I mean a man and his wife stopped, and he
changed the tire, and they said I was lucky.

"They're doing work along that stretch of the
road, and I could easily have crashed through the
flimsy barrier they put up. Then I would have gone
down an embankment.

"The tire was so bad I just left it there on the
shoulder of the road.''

I was disappointed. "It's too bad you don't have
the tire. Maybe somebody could look at it and tell
whether it had been tampered with—or something."
I didn't know much about tires, but a garage me-
chanic should know. The tire would have been
evidence.

Charlene shook her head. "The tire was a mess.
Badly torn up. Nobody could have told anything
from that tire."

"Maybe David knew it would be like that," I said darkly.

We considered that for a moment, and Charlene sighed forlornly. "Oh, it's just too much for me, Marjorie. And I'm probably wrong. It was just a coincidence that David took the train and I had a blow-out driving in. It was just a coincidence, wasn't it?"

She didn't sound very convinced.

"I guess it could be." I knew I didn't sound very convinced either. I was jittery with the scary excitement of being thrust into such an amazing situation as sitting in my cousin's luxurious living room talking about her husband trying to murder her. It was the last thing in the world I would have expected to happen to me, ever.

"It's just like the letter said," I whispered. It seemed a time for whispering, there in the shadowy early twilight of the rainy, rainy day. " 'He has already tried—' " I quoted from the letter, and immediately fresh questions came to mind. "Whoever wrote the letters knows that David tried to kill you once. But how could that be? How could anyone know that?"

Charlene stared at me helplessly. Finally she said, "Maybe—maybe he has an accomplice. I don't know. I'm just so confused. No, it wouldn't be an accomplice. An accomplice would be on David's side, and whoever wrote the letters is trying to warn me about David."

"Well, it's *somebody*," I insisted. "Somebody

who thinks that David murdered Rosemary, and who also knows about that time you had the car accident. Maybe—maybe somebody in David's family."

"He hasn't any family around here," Charlene said, putting an end to that idea. "He doesn't have much family at all, actually. His parents are dead. They were originally from Canada, and I think there are a few cousins still there. But David hasn't seen them for years."

"Let's go to the police," I said impulsively, but Charlene held up her hand to stop me before I had the sentence finished.

"I can't go to the police, Marjorie," she said with a stricken expression. "David is my husband, I *love* him. I'm sure Rosemary's death was an accident, and the tire blow-out probably was too. I wouldn't want David to think I was so quick to suspect him."

I thought it would be much more thrilling to rush off to the police station. I knew David so slightly that it was easy for me to move him around to play different parts. Husband. Businessman. Murderer. I had to remind myself that he was the most important person in Charlene's life, a husband she loved, a person she had lived with for three years and never had had reason to suspect of anything.

"We'll just bide our time," she said with an air of decision. "We'll see if any more letters come before we go to the police. And this is still just between the two of us. Okay?"

I felt regretful that we weren't going to do something more dramatic than just bide our time, but I said okay.

    The evening seemed to last forever.

    What would the morning mail bring?

    We decided to go to bed early, and Charlene said, "Let's hope tomorrow will be better." By which she meant she hoped there wouldn't be any more letters.

    The rain was still falling when we went to bed. I don't know what time that night it stopped.

Chapter Eight

THERE WAS NO LETTER IN THE MAIL THE next morning. At least not the letter we were watching for. Charlene shuffled through the envelopes twice. "Ads—ads—oh, it's just junk mail and an electric bill."

She tossed it all aside on the patio table.

I suppose I should have felt grateful, but the absence of a new letter left me with a restless, dissatisfied feeling. The second letter had said so much more than the first, and I had been hoping that a third letter—if there was one—would say even more, maybe give us some clue about who wrote the letters.

If there was going to be a third letter, we would have to wait for it. I didn't see how I could stand the suspense. Mom said I always wanted things to happen *now*. But what was wrong with that, I always asked her.

Although the sky was still overcast, the garden had a vivid greenness after the rain of the day before. The flagstones were dark and damp. Raindrops still clung to the leaves of the trees and a squirrel darting from a tree branch sent a shower into the air.

"I hope to heaven it doesn't rain anymore," Charlene said with a sudden burst of emotion. "I don't need this depressing weather on top of everything else."

She tapped her fingers on the rejected mail and frowned at the sodden garden. She didn't say anything about what fun thing we'd do that day. I thought maybe she'd forgotten I was even there.

"Did you save that second letter?" I asked, to remind her that I was there and ready to help if I could. "It's evidence, you know."

She had torn the first letter into pieces, and it was too late to do anything about that now. I thought it would be a good thing to hang on to the second letter. Maybe there wouldn't be a third.

"I saved it," she admitted. "It seems disloyal to David, but I did save it."

"That's good," I said, trying to sound helpful.

"I've got to get away from here," Charlene said grimly. "Away from here and away from these damned letters."

I thought she meant something like a movie, or shopping.

"I ought to just get in the car this minute and go up to the lake."

I was surprised, but it certainly sounded like an exciting and dramatic thing to do.

"Really, Charlene? I've been dying to see that house."

"Then let's do it." Charlene turned from the garden to look at me intently. "Let's just get in the car and go up there for a couple of days. We can always go back again with David when he gets home from his trip."

I had a fleeting moment of wondering how much I would like to be at a secluded lake cottage with David—when the time came. But Charlene was rushing on. "It's just what we need. We'll go this afternoon," she said decisively.

"We can go this morning if you want to." I wanted to do everything I could to help her. "I can be ready in ten minutes."

Which was an exaggeration, but not much. I would have been willing to try anyway.

Charlene smiled faintly at my eagerness. "Well, *I* couldn't be ready in ten minutes," she said. "There are things to take care of if we're going to be away. And there's the packing. We can do all that, and go right after lunch. It's only about a four-and-a-half-hour drive. We'll be there long before dark."

"Great!" I said. "What shall I pack for? Two days? Three days?"

"Three. Why not?" Charlene made an expansive

motion with her hands. "Oh, it will be *so good* to get away."

The morning seemed silent after the steady sound of rain the day before. The overcast sky closed down around the house and shrouded it even more in oppressive stillness.

The phone rang a couple of times, sounding shrill and loud. The first time, I heard Charlene talking to one of her friends who was calling to thank her for the lunch. The second time the phone rang I was already upstairs in my room deciding what clothes to take to the lake. When I ran downstairs to get something, Charlene was just hanging up the phone. "That was David," she said. "Just calling to say hello. I told him we were going to the lake for a couple of days."

When we talked on the patio that morning Charlene was anxious to go to the lake. By twelve o'clock, as I was packing the last things into my suitcase, she came to the door of my room and said we weren't going after all.

"I've lost all track of days," she said wearily as she came into the room and sat down on the corner of my bed. "I didn't realize it was Friday." She had just come from the shower, and I could smell the lily-of-the-valley bath oil she always used. She was wearing a loose summer robe, her hair tied back with a narrow pink ribbon.

My suitcase was open on the bed, and she looked at it absently.

"Traffic is so heavy going toward the resort areas on Friday afternoons. This dreadful headache of mine is back. I just want to lie down and rest. I couldn't cope with the traffic, not this afternoon."

I guess I looked pretty surprised, because right away she said, "Oh, we're going to the lake. I *have* to get away for a few days. We'll go tomorrow. I'm just not up to driving there today. I have to lie down until my headache lets up."

I couldn't offer to do the driving for her. Driver's ed. still lay ahead for me my next year at school. I was looking forward to the classes with mixed feelings. Driving would be great in a million ways. But would I be good enough? Could I squeeze into parking places where only Eddie Jackson and boys like him could maneuver cars? Could I ease onto expressways without causing a ten-car pile-up? Could I manage through Indiana's snowy, icy winters?

Charlene rubbed her hand across her aching forehead and said, "Yes, I just want to rest awhile." I had the feeling that something had happened. I couldn't imagine what, but something had happened to change our plans. Charlene had been *so* anxious to get away, to go to the lake. Were a headache and heavy traffic really enough to make her want to wait a whole day?

Something was wrong, I was sure.

"Did you get another letter?" I blurted out without thinking. How could she get another letter? The letter carrier had come and gone. There was only one mail delivery. He wouldn't be back until the next morning. There was no logical way Charlene could have received a letter.

Unless it had come some other way. A special delivery. Or an envelope shoved under the door. That must be it.

"You got another letter, didn't you," I said. It wasn't even a question. I was stating fact. I was *so sure*.

Charlene looked at me warily. "Another letter? No, how could I have gotten another letter?"

I felt frustrated again. Of course there was no letter. I was jumping to conclusions beyond reason. But *something* was wrong. I didn't know what it was. There was no way I could have known. But I puzzled over it after Charlene left to go to her room and rest.

Whatever had happened, we weren't leaving for the lake until the next day. At least we would be at home in the morning to see if another letter arrived. I thought of that with some consolation.

By evening Charlene said her headache was gone. "Thank heaven," she added dramatically. The day had been long and gloomy for both of us. We phoned for pizza—which is a pretty good way to cheer up any gloomy day—and I was in the kitchen watching Charlene toss a salad when the delivery boy came. Charlene was big on salads. I knew Mom would be happy that I was "eating right."

It was about six o'clock and already growing

dusky. Another short day because of cloudy skies. But at least there had been no more rain. The evening was turning cool, and the pizza smelled wonderful, even through the cardboard carton.

Charlene paid the boy, and I went to the patio with placemats and napkins. When I came back I heard her dialing the phone in the hall.

"I thought I'd call David and let him know we didn't get to the lake today after all," she said to me.

That seemed perfectly logical to me. I bustled about, transferring the pizza to a large cookie sheet so we could keep it warm in the oven while we ate our salad. Then I got silverware and plates and finished setting the patio table. As I moved back and forth from kitchen to patio I could hear Charlene talking to David.

"We're going tomorrow, probably about noon. . . . Just for a couple of days. We have those tickets for the play Tuesday. We should drive back Monday. I told Marjorie we can go back to the lake when you get home, just as we planned. . . ."

Through the oven's glass door I could see the electric coils glowing red, keeping our pizza warm. I found extra oregano in the cupboard.

"Yes, I remember Charlie Denton. . . . Okay, I'll let you get on your way. Enjoy your dinner."

Charlene hung up the phone and smoothed her hair. "Well, David sounds just fine," she said hopefully. "Hearing his voice makes those letters seem even more preposterous than ever. He was late to meet a business friend for dinner, so I let him go. Otherwise you could have said hello."

I was glad I didn't have to talk to David. I never know what to say on long-distance phone calls, and I hardly knew David. Sometimes my aunt Dorothy called from California and I'd answer the phone. If I'd have known it was long distance, I'd have let Mom or Dad answer. But there I was, stuck having to think of something to say to an aunt I had only met once in my whole life when I was ten years old. It was always awkward.

I tried to look disappointed, but I was secretly thankful that there wasn't time for me to talk to David. It would be hard enough talking to him when he came back from the business trip. I would be wondering about his first wife drowning and about the blown-out tire Charlene had had.

How could I make casual conversation with him?

At least I had a few more days before I'd have to face that problem.

Chapter Nine

WHEN I ASKED CHARLENE WHAT TIME WE would be leaving for the lake house on Saturday, she said, "Oh, about noon." Nothing like my mom and dad, who are always departing at dawn, whether they're going to Italy or for a weekend at my grandma's house in Fort Wayne.

Charlene liked to sleep late if she could. Also, I thought, she wanted to wait for the mail. It usually came about ten o'clock, but sometimes later.

We might as well not have waited. There was no third mysterious anonymous letter in the Saturday morning mail.

The cloudy weather was ending. As we moved about the house doing last-minute things, pale sunlight crept across the garden. A breeze ruffled the white petunias, and a cluster of sparrows twittered on the garden walk.

I watered Charlene's house plants and programmed the VCR to record a movie while we were away.

For lunch we finished the leftover pizza from the night before. Most of the things in the refrigerator would keep the few days we would be gone. Two cantaloupes and a box of strawberries we stuffed into a bag to take with us.

"There's a grocery in Crossing," Charlene told me. "That's a little town near the cottage. We can stop there and get the other things we'll need."

She looked tired. There were faint dark circles under her eyes, and a drawn look around her mouth. I hoped she would feel better when we got to the lake house.

We left Larrimore Hills at twelve-thirty. It was a four- or five-hour drive to the lake house, depending on traffic, and we stopped for a snack about three o'clock at an expressway restaurant, which was large, impersonal, bright with chrome, and only sparsely filled at that hour of the afternoon. I had a milk shake and Charlene had coffee.

The air-conditioning was turned too high, and the restaurant was cold.

While Charlene paid the check, I twirled a revolving rack of souvenir postcards and saw scenes of Buckingham Fountain, Sears Tower, and the Chicago skyline at night. Sights we certainly didn't have in Sanderville, Indiana.

Charlene had gotten tickets to a play in Chicago

for Tuesday night, when we would be back from the lake house. We were going into the city for the day and I was looking forward to sightseeing. Trixie and I sure would have opposite things to talk about when we got together again. She'd have camping-in-the-woods stories, and I'd have Chicago ones.

"Ready to go?" Charlene was beside me, putting away the change she'd gotten from the cashier.

"All ready," I said, giving the postcard rack another last twirl. No, we didn't have anything like those pictures in Sanderville.

Back in the car, I traced our progress on the roadmap Charlene had in the glove compartment. We had circled the lower end of Lake Michigan, through Indiana, and were then in Michigan heading north along the lake. A short time after we left the restaurant, we turned off the expressway. The lake cottage was near Grand Haven, and our way now led through scenic wooded areas, past small towns and summer resorts.

The afternoon had grown hot, but we were enclosed in Charlene's midnight-blue, air-conditioned car. We swept along in cool luxury, with music playing on the radio. Charlene's hands rested lightly on the steering wheel; thin silver bracelets slid back from her wrist and her fingertips kept time to the radio music.

A stretch of roadway that ran parallel with a stream reminded me of Trixie. At one spot several men stood at the streamside, fishing.

"I bet Trixie's at that place White Wood where

her dad wants to fish," I said to Charlene, turning my head to look out of the car window at the men by the stream. Green light of the trees overshadowing the men filtered down on their shoulders and caps. There was a calmness about them, a patience, as the water of the stream flowed by and they held their fishing poles.

"It's nice to have a best freind," Charlene said when I mentioned Trixie. Taking her eyes off the road long enough to look over at me, she smiled. "My best friend in high school was a girl named Gwen. Maybe you remember her? Gwen Avery. She was kind of a tall girl, with gorgeous red hair. Her father owned the furniture store on Clinton Street. They had a lot of money. I was always jealous of Gwen."

I thought it was odd to be jealous of a best friend. It was a contradiction of feelings, wasn't it, to be jealous of a best friend?

Ahead, the roadway flew toward us. Trees dappled the hood of the car with sunlight. Music floated out from the radio and Charlene's fingers tapped time on the steering wheel. I was glad we were off the expressway: the big trucks made me nervous.

"Whatever I had, Gwen had something better," Charlene said with a shrug. "But we always had fun together. She was my best friend."

Something stirred deep in my memory, and I had a fleeting impression of a warm, cozy room where snow was falling at the window, an impression of something shiny whirling round and round, and snow melting on the floor. An impression gone as suddenly as it had come, so quickly I didn't even have time to wonder about it.

"What happened to her?" I asked. "Isn't she still your best friend?"

Charlene shook her head. "That was way back in high school. We've gone our separate ways."

"Didn't you keep in touch?" I was concerned. Maybe Trixie and I would end up living far apart because of jobs or marriage or whatever; but we would always write letters and visit each other and stuff like that. I couldn't imagine Trixie just fading out of my life forever.

"That's the way it goes most of the time." Charlene's tone was nonchalant. "Gwen's father sold the furniture store and the family moved away. I've never seen her since."

I thought that was sad.

"Who's your best friend now?" I asked.

Charlene moved her head back and forth to show indecision. "I have lots of friends in Larrimore Hills. I don't know exactly which one would be 'best.' They're all nice."

She didn't really sound enthused about any of her friends in Larrimore Hills, and I had a sudden thought: "You miss Sanderville, don't you?"

I couldn't have been more wrong.

"Miss Sanderville?" Charlene rolled her eyes theatrically. "I *never* want to go back to that dreary old place."

I was a little hurt at how emphatically she said

that. I could see for myself that Larrimore Hills, with its luxurious homes, lying in the shadow of a big, exciting city like Chicago, was a lot different from Sanderville, Indiana, which was kind of out in the middle of nowhere special. But Sanderville didn't deserve to be put down so completely. It was a pretty town, a pretty place to live. Indiana in general was a pretty place to live.

"I sort of like Sanderville," I said loyally. I wanted very much to be like Charlene, to look like her, act like her, *be* like her. I thought everything she did was wonderful. But I had to stick up for Sanderville.

"I'll give you a couple more years, and you won't be able to get out of there fast enough," Charlene said with assurance.

That's what she had done. She had come home from college and then left almost immediately to live in Chicago. She and a girlfriend from college had an apartment for a while, until Charlene married David. And the rest was history, as they say. Or at least the rest was marriage, money, and Larrimore Hills.

"Believe me," Charlene said, her eyes on the road as it curved through the woods, "someday you won't be able to get out of Sanderville fast enough."

The fishing stream lay behind us now, the patient men with their fishing poles long gone. The road was surrounded by forest, by trees close together on both sides. When I tried to look between the trees, there was only darkness.

I thought about our house on Westen Street in Sanderville—a nice ordinary house, painted white with a black slate roof and rose trellises along the south wall. Across the street was the Donahue house, that I knew as well as my own. Trixie's mother had two cats: a dainty small white cat and a sorrowful-looking yellow cat with only one ear. They sat in the window and kept watch over Westen Street, rain or shine. I suppose I thought of them right then because they were so much a part of Westen Street, as much a part as old Mrs. Philby who could always be seen chewing twigs from bushes as she worked in her garden, or Benny Willis who always came zooming home with his car radio blaring loud enough to be heard in Indianapolis.

I thought about school and all my friends there.

I thought about Eddie Jackson.

I wondered if Charlene was right and I would someday want to get away from Sanderville. If I would someday lose track of Trixie, as Charlene had lost track of Gwen Avery.

Gwen Avery . . . Something nudged my memory again.

"I remember something about Gwen," I said slowly, watching the woods unfold ahead of us, not sure exactly what it was I remembered.

"You do?" Charlene glanced over at me with surprise. "You were pretty little when Gwen and I were friends."

"I know. But I do remember her—and—and didn't she have some problem with a boyfriend, or something like that?" Things blurred together indistinctly in my mind. But there was something about Gwen. There was *something*.

The car whizzed along. Charlene's silver bracelets glistened in the flashes of sunlight that slanted across the road.

"I don't remember anything like that," she said. "Gwen had lots of boyfriends, but I don't recall any special problem. All the boys liked her."

I thought about Eddie Jackson, and I wished I were a girl all the boys liked.

Chapter Ten

IT WAS ABOUT FIVE O'CLOCK WHEN WE
reached Crossing, a secluded resort town appearing
as if by magic out of the wooded landscape.

"I'll give you a tour," Charlene offered, heading
the car down a quiet street. "Then we'll have dinner
at a darling place I know, and after that we can pick
up some groceries to take on to the house."

She was so sweet in her eagerness to show me the
pretty little town, I forgave her for putting down
Sanderville so rudely. And maybe she was right.
Maybe a time would come when I would want to get
as far away as I could from small-town life. Living
in a big city or living in a fancy suburb like Larrimore Hills was probably lots of fun.

As I watched the streets of Crossing glide by, I

thought it would also be fun to live in a resort town nestled between the woods and sandy dunes that gleamed white in the sunlight.

"Most of the houses along here are just summer places." Charlene motioned to the houses we were passing. Here and there a car with a motorboat attached was parked in a driveway. In one side yard children's bathing suits were drying on a clothesline strung between two trees.

"On up ahead here you'll see some terrific houses, year-round houses—the owners are all millionaires."

Charlene turned into a street that was broader and more impressive, and we began to pass large houses sheltered by hedges, iron fences, and brick walls overhung with shade trees. Sprawled upon well-cared-for lawns, the houses beyond the hedges and fences and brick walls looked magnificent.

"Look, they're playing croquet." Charlene called my attention to a group gathered on the front lawn of one of the houses. Our car crawled past, and I saw girls about my age, wearing shorts, batting wooden balls at croquet wickets stuck into the grass. We couldn't hear anything, with the car windows rolled up and the air-conditioning going, but I could tell they were having fun. I thought if the girls had been closer and our car windows had been open, we would have heard the sound of laughter mixed with the clunk of wooden mallets against wooden balls.

Lake Michigan, glimpsed between houses and

trees as we reached the end of the wide street, seemed to stretch away into a far, far distance.

There was no end to it, no seeing across to the other side; just a vast calm body of water to the horizon.

It was a perfect afternoon for sailing, and there were sailboats on the lake. Motorboat trails ruffled the waters near shore. Farthest out of all was some kind of large boat, maybe somebody's yacht, I thought, or a sight-seeing boat. Mom and Dad had been on a sight-seeing cruise once when they were in Chicago, with dinner and dancing right on the boat.

"How close is your house to the lake?" I was more eager than ever to see Charlene and David's cottage. I had never realized a *big* lake could be so fascinating. I thought it was probably the biggest lake in the whole world.

"We're pretty close to the lake," Charlene said. "You can see a bit of it from the kitchen window, and you can walk there in just a minute. There's a little trail that goes through the woods. Oh, maybe it would be a block if you were in town."

It sounded wonderful to me.

By and by we came to the town square, surrounded with small shops, the Crossing Public Library, and the town hall with a statue of a man on a horse in front.

The restaurant Charlene had in mind was across the square from the post office, where a flag fluttered in the sunlight.

Home Cooking was promised by an elaborately lettered sign in the front window of the restaurant. It was a small place, designed like an old-fashioned dining room with plate rails and waitresses in long skirts and white ruffled caps.

"David and I love this place," Charlene confided as we settled ourselves at a table. "We come here a lot, when I don't feel like cooking."

We were early for the dinner hour, but people began to come in as we ate. By six o'clock all of the tables were occupied.

When we left the restaurant, we walked across the square and down the street a block or so to a grocery store. We wanted milk and a few other things to take to the house. It was while we were in the grocery store that what I was trying to remember about Charlene's girlfriend Gwen came back to me. Charlene had disappeared momentarily around the end of the grocery store aisle, and I found myself staring at a shelf of cake mixes. I saw in my mind my mom's big yellow mixing bowl on a kitchen table back home in Sanderville. Charlene was making a cake. She was baby-sitting me and she was going to let me help make a cake. She had the box of cake mix open, we were all ready, I could hardly wait.

It was snowing outside, and the kitchen was warm and snug and bright. I watched Charlene pouring the cake mix into the bowl in a powdery chocolate stream.

"You can beat the eggs, honey," Charlene said to

me. She gave the eggbeater a twirl and the shiny metal blades spun around with a rattling sound. I was going to beat the eggs. It was a very important part of making the cake.

How old was I? Six? No, more—seven, maybe.

And then someone came in. A girl with red hair, all cold and snowy. She pulled Charlene away from the table where we were going to make our cake. "You knew how much I liked him. You knew it. Why didn't you leave him alone?"

The girl began to cry, and I saw that the snow on her boots was melting on the kitchen floor, but she didn't notice.

"Go and play, Marjorie," Charlene said to me. She forgot all about our cake.

"I want to beat the eggs." But Charlene didn't listen to me.

The girl with the red hair cried and kept saying, "How could you do that to me, how could you be so mean?"

"I didn't know you liked him."

"Yes, you did, you did."

Charlene turned on me angrily. "Go and play, Marjorie. I told you to go play."

I was frightened suddenly as Charlene shouted at me, and I ran away from the kitchen. . . .

I felt a little unsettled as I stood there in the Crossing grocery store remembering that time so far away and long ago. Seeing so clearly the snow falling, the yellow bowl on the table, as though I were in that kitchen right then.

Charlene had told me she didn't remember any special problem with Gwen and a boyfriend. Could she really have forgotten it? *I* had remembered it all these years, and when I thought of it now it made me uneasy and unhappy.

I moved on slowly, pushing the grocery cart Charlene had left in my charge. I knew she was somewhere just around the next aisle. I thought I wouldn't say anything to her about what I remembered. But it would have been nice if she had kept in touch with Gwen and we could know that Gwen had found other boys to like and was happy wherever she was now. Her heart had been broken that long-ago day, I knew that for sure.

It was nearly seven when we left the town and started on the last lap of our trip.

Charlene said it was about twenty minutes from Crossing to the cottage.

Most of the way was along a winding road through woods which were still filled with the last long slanting rays of summer evening sunlight.

Crossing slipped into the distance behind us, and I thought the croquet girls were gone from the lawn now, and little children had been called in from play on the sandy beaches and were getting ready for bed.

Chapter Eleven

THE LAKE HOUSE WAS ON A RISE OF ground that was almost completely hidden from the road by trees. We parked the car by a flight of wooden steps built into the hillside and climbed the steps to the house.

The sun was setting and the road was already deep in shadow, but streaks of light came through the trees and into the living room.

"Welcome to the Kensington summer estate," Charlene said with a playful flourish as we went in.

There was a fieldstone fireplace, and comfortable-looking furniture upholstered in beige and olive green. Windows looked out to the porch that surrounded the front and one side of the house.

"It's great!" I set down my suitcase and looked around at everything. At one side of the living room, a stairway went up to a gallery that over-looked the living room. Bedrooms led off from it.

"Do you really use the fireplace?" I hadn't ex-pected to see a fireplace in a summer house.

"Sometimes the nights get chilly here," Charlene said. "Specially if we come up early in the season, or in the autumn. It's beautiful here in the woods in September and October, but the nights get cold." She tossed her purse on a chair by the fireplace and beckoned me to follow her. "Come on, I'll show you the kitchen."

The house faced the road, and it was from the kitchen window at the back that we could just see the lake through the trees. The last daylight glim-mered on the waters. "We have a little pier, but you can't see it from here," Charlene said as we stood at the kitchen window. "We'll go down first thing in the morning and have a swim."

She switched on the kitchen light and tried the faucets at the sink.

"We haven't been up here for a few weeks," she explained. "And I always like to check to be sure everything's in order."

Water streamed from the faucets.

"Okay." Charlene twisted the faucets and the water stopped. "Would you run back to the car and get that bag of groceries? Then you can lock it up, okay?" She tossed me the keys. Feeling important and thrilled with the idea of being at a house in the woods by a lake, I ran back through the living room, down the porch steps and the hillside to get the groceries.

By now the woods and roadway were lost in dusk. Everything was silent. No cars went by. The woods were hushed, the birds quiet. I checked to be sure all the car windows were rolled up, although there did not seem any chance of rain that night. Then I locked the car and carried the grocery bag up the steps to the house. Charlene was still in the kitchen. When I came in, she turned from a cupboard which she had just opened.

"I thought we had more canned goods here—and the coffee's just about gone."

I stood irresolutely, and then I set the bag down on the counter by the sink. "I don't drink coffee," I reminded her. "You can have all of it."

She shrugged. "We can get some tomorrow. I just thought there was more here." She took the things I was unpacking from the grocery bag and began to tuck them away, some in the cupboard, some in the refrigerator. I put the oranges in an empty fruit basket that was on the kitchen table.

When the bag was empty, Charlene said, "Come on, we can take a quick look at the lake while it's still light enough to see something."

We went along the path toward the lake. The trees thinned out and there was a short stretch of sandy shore and the beautiful lake stretching to the horizon—large as an ocean to my eyes. There were no sailboats or motorboats in sight then, just the expanse of dark water lapping peacefully in the sunset.

We walked to the pier, and stood there watching the last light on the lake.

I thought about how super it would be to live by a lake and how lucky Charlene was to have this nice place to come to in the summers. Far out on the lake was a light, and I watched it, wondering what boat it shone from and what the people were doing who were out there.

I liked the woods too. Maybe camping would be more fun than I had thought. Maybe I was an outdoor girl all along, and I hadn't known it. Charlene and I would probably take hikes through the woods . . .

Suddenly Charlene turned and peered back toward the trees. "What was that?"

"What was what?" I followed her gaze, but there was nothing to see except the trees, dark against the twilight sky. We couldn't even see the house through the trees.

Charlene seemed to be listening to something for a moment, and then she relaxed and shrugged her shoulders. "Nothing, I guess. I thought I heard something. It was probably only a squirrel or a rabbit."

"I hope that's all the wildlife you have around here," I said, joking as we left the pier and started back toward the house.

"We saw a deer once," Charlene said. "But mostly it's just squirrels and birds. The people down the road have a couple of dogs, but we hardly ever see them."

Something about the way she tilted her head made me think she was still listening for sounds in the woods.

"Did you hear something else?" I asked. All I could hear was the sound of our own footsteps as we occasionally crushed a twig or leaf on the path.

"No, no—" She lifted her hand and brushed my question aside.

As we got closer to the house we could see the kitchen light gleaming through the trees, looking bright and cozy in the darkening woods.

"Now you can see the rest of the house," Charlene said, holding the door open into the bright kitchen for me. "Let's get our suitcases and carry them upstairs."

The daylight had faded completely now. The living room had grown dark.

"The room you'll be sleeping in has a nice view of the lake—" Charlene's voice stopped as she flicked a wall switch back and forth and the living room remained dark.

She went across the dark room and tried the lamps at either end of the sofa, then the lamp on the table by the front windows. I stood in the kitchen-living room doorway, watching her move about the room, a dim figure in the light coming from the kitchen.

"None of these lights work," she said with exasperation. "This is just great."

"What's wrong with them?" I came a step or two into the room.

"We've had trouble with fuses," Charlene said. "I'll have a look at the fuse box. Will you run upstairs and see if the lights are working in the bedrooms? I'm not sure what other rooms are on the same circuit as the living room."

Just barely enough fading light came through the windows for me to manage to go up the stairway to the gallery above the living room. The bedroom doors were open, and I heard Charlene call from below, "Light switches are on the right-hand side by the doors."

But there wasn't a light working in the whole upstairs. The windows in the bedrooms were blurry with shadows from the trees growing close to the house, and I had the horrible, nightmarish feeling that something might jump out at me from behind an unfamiliar piece of furniture looming in the dark rooms.

I could easily tell which room was the bathroom. The bathtub and washbasin were ghostly white figures in the gloom. No light switch working there. Maybe something was hiding . . .

It was with relief that I started downstairs again, holding the banister and making my way carefully.

Charlene was in a little hallway at one side of the kitchen, and I could see a light on in a small bathroom off the hall.

"Nothing working upstairs," I reported apologetically. I would have liked to bring her better news.

"Thank heaven this bathroom is on the kitchen circuit," Charlene said. She had the door of a small wall compartment open, and I could see the round ends of fuses all in a row. I was glad she knew how to change fuses. I certainly didn't.

But there were no fuses to replace the bad ones. We rummaged through the drawer in the kitchen where Charlene said fuses were always kept. We found a flashlight, twine, kitchen matches, a screwdriver and a hammer, odds and ends of things, but no fuses. We looked in other kitchen drawers, the silverware drawer, the towel drawer, the knife and utensil drawer, where fuses couldn't possibly be. "This is ridiculous," Charlene kept saying. "We have a whole *box* of fuses. David is always very particular about things like that. He's a methodical, reliable, organized person—now there must be some fuses here someplace."

But there were no fuses.

We went into the little hallway and examined the fuse box again, helplessly. Being at a summer house with no lights, except for the kitchen, a tiny hallway, and a small bathroom, wasn't a whole lot of fun. We'd have to go out to get fuses. There must be some store open in Crossing where we could get fuses.

It wasn't the end of the world, but I had a frustrating sense of something gone wrong that I wanted to change but couldn't.

Charlene slammed shut the door of the fuse compartment.

"I knew it, I just knew it would happen sometime," she said with a burst of nervous anger. "Someone's *been* here, I know it!"

"What do you mean, someone's been here?" I gaped at her with dismay.

"Been here, been here," she repeated impatiently. "Broken in while we were away." She swept her blond hair back from her forehead with a distracted gesture. "I didn't want to scare you, but—well, look what I picked up by the back door as we came from the pier."

She reached into the pocket of her skirt and held out an empty cigarette package, crumpled but new looking.

"It was right by the kitchen door, like somebody stood there on the back steps and took out the last cigarette and threw down this empty pack. And I know there was coffee, there was a *lot* of coffee last time we were here." She flung open cupboard doors and motioned inside. "Look! The soup's gone—the canned tomato juice. Someone's *been* here and either took the food away to eat someplace else or cooked it here and cleaned up so we wouldn't know. Yes, yes, look," she said. "That's not where we keep pans! They should be on the other shelf—"

I stared blankly into cupboards where food was missing and cooking pots misplaced. I could feel my heart beginning to beat faster.

"How could someone get in?" I got the words out breathlessly.

Charlene left the cupboard doors hanging open and began to examine the back door. She opened it and stared at the doorknob and the lock above it.

"Come here, Marjorie. Look. Someone tried to get in this way."

I went closer and I could see gouge marks in the wood, as if someone was trying to wedge something into the door and pry the lock. It gave me a prickly feeling along my arms to see the crude, jabbed marks around the door lock.

"Maybe he's still around," I whispered, thinking in panic of how Charlene had thought she heard something when we were standing by the pier.

Charlene closed the kitchen door and clicked the lock into place. It was working. She jiggled the knob and tugged at the door, but it stayed locked. Somehow, I wasn't all that reassured. "Maybe whoever it was is still here," I said again, glancing up to indicate the dark bedrooms above.

Charlene stared at me for a moment. Then she turned away from the door and sank down into a chair at the kitchen table. She put her arms out in front of her on the table, and her slender fingers picked at the woven rim of the straw fruit basket where I had put the oranges.

"There's never been any problem around here, it's always been peaceful and safe." She looked up at me gravely. "I don't know what to think."

I felt too jumpy to sit down, so I stood by the table and watched her fuss nervously with the basket rim. Then she pushed it away impatiently and drew her arms close, as though she were cold.

"It just gives me a scary feeling to think someone, some stranger, has been right here in this very room."

She shivered and glanced around the kitchen.

Yes, it does give you a scary feeling. It certainly gave *me* a scary feeling. And I was still worried about those dark rooms upstairs. *Anybody* could be hiding there. Maybe that's why the lights wouldn't work and the fuses were gone: so we wouldn't see who it was in the darkness. And then what would happen when we were asleep at night? Would we be murdered in our sleep? I wouldn't be, because I wasn't going to sleep!

Suddenly Charlene twisted her head toward the kitchen window.

"What was that noise?"

We stared at the window, which Charlene had opened when we first arrived. Then she said softly, "Turn out the light, Marjorie."

The light switch was on the wall by the door, the gouged-up door. My fingers flew to it, and the room was instantly dark. I heard Charlene's chair move against the floor as she stood up.

Together we huddled by the window, staring into the woods.

The sunset was over. The last afterglow was gone from the sky. Darkness was descending on the woods and shore and lake. We stared fearfully into the woods beyond the house, searching for some sign of movement. Then Charlene whispered, "Something moved out there. Look, Marjorie, over by the big tree at the edge of the path. Someone's there."

Chapter Twelve

DO YOU SEE HIM, MARJORIE?" I FELT Charlene's hand touch my arm. Her fingers were cold.

"Yes, I see him." My voice sounded strained and tight, not like my real voice at all. Just where Charlene had said, I saw something move between the trees. Something large. No squirrel or rabbit or dog. Something much larger than that. Something as large as a man.

Then, panicky, I drew back from the window to put as much distance between me and whomever—whatever—was moving out there between the trees.

"We shouldn't stay here," I said urgently to Charlene. "We should just get in the car and get out of here."

Charlene moved back from the window too. She didn't say anything for a few moments, and I waited, feeling shaky and wishing I were a million miles away.

Finally Charlene said, "I think you're right, Marjorie. We shouldn't stay here—but—"

"But what?"

"It's going to be completely dark in just a few minutes. And it can get *so* dark in the woods at night. You don't know how dark. And desolate. There wouldn't be much other traffic. I just don't like the idea of it."

I didn't either. I thought of roads twisting through lonely forest places, lighted ahead only as far as the beam of our own headlights. All around us, darkness. What if we had car trouble? We would be helpless in those dark woods.

"Maybe we could go as far as the town, as far as Crossing," I said impulsively. "There must be a hotel there or something, some place where we could stay until morning."

I thought it was a great idea. Mostly, I just wanted to get away from the lake house, from the woods, from whatever was in the woods.

"Maybe we could do that—go to town," Charlene said cautiously. I knew she was thinking it over, deciding what to do. I couldn't even drive the car! I felt frustrated, trapped—everything depended on what Charlene decided.

She moved back toward the window, and I stayed close beside her nervously.

"There *is* someone there," she whispered after staring intently toward the woods. She caught her breath sharply. "I think there are two of them."

I was frozen with fear. Two? *Two?* Now that we had decided to leave and go to town, we probably wouldn't even be able to make it to the car. Even if we were brave enough to make a dash for the car, it would be more an act of madness than bravery.

I drew close to Charlene again, peering through the window screen. With darkness, the woods had drawn in closer about the house. Every tree branch vibrated with menace. It was almost totally dark; night had fallen around us.

"We'll call the police," Charlene said decisively. I could hear the thin edge of panic in her voice. "And there's a gun here somewhere—in the living room, I think."

She moved past me in the darkness of the kitchen, and I heard her footsteps crossing the floor of the living room. There was the sound of a drawer sliding open.

"Here it is."

I stood in the dark kitchen, knowing that Charlene had gone into the living room and found a gun.

Guns had not played a large part in my life.

They had played no part.

I stood halfway between the kitchen window and the living-room doorway and felt my mouth go dry and my throat close up.

As I made my way toward the doorway, I heard

Charlene lift the phone from its cradle. I thought of how at the other end was a good, strong, wonderful police department with brave men to come and rescue us.

But something was wrong. I heard Charlene frantically jiggling the button on the phone. "Marjorie, there's no dial tone, nothing. The phone's dead."

I stood in the kitchen doorway, feeling as if I were in a horror movie or the middle of a nightmare.

"Try again," I urged. My throat was so tight it was hard to speak.

I heard Charlene jiggle the button, trying to get a response.

There was none.

Chapter Thirteen

DO YOU THINK THEY CUT THE WIRES OUT-side?" I felt my way through the dark toward Charlene.

"Yes, I suppose they did."

I heard her put down the phone.

"But why?" I was trembling. Charlene didn't answer. I knew she was as frightened as I was.

As we stood there, confused and helpless, I remembered the article I had read in the newspaper about the man who escaped from the mental institution. Even though I knew that had happened hundreds of miles away, and the man had surely been captured by then, I still thought of the two menacing figures in the woods as desperate, insane men who would murder us.

I knew we didn't dare leave the house now. We

were prisoners, and without the phone there was no way to get help.

Charlene was thinking about this too.

"Maybe we could make a run for the car," she said uncertainly. I could see her silhouetted against a front window.

"It's so dark," I said, thinking of the flight of steps down the hillside. How could I manage them? "I don't know if—"

"Wait—" Charlene interrupted me with a harsh whisper. "There's someone over there by those trees at the end of the porch."

Yes! Yes! I saw the stealthy movement in the dark. One was at the back of the house, and one was at the front. Unless there were more than two. How many were there?

"Do you see him?" Charlene whispered, and I whispered back, cold with fear, "Yes, yes. Oh, what will we do?"

"There's an outside light," Charlene said. "If it's still working. It's at the top of the hill steps."

"See if it works," I whispered. Anything seemed better than trying to peer into the darkness of the night. "Maybe it will scare them away."

Charlene pressed a switch by the door, and an outdoor light, like a small street lamp, glowed in the darkness beyond the porch, at the top of the wooden stairway leading down to the road. The light barely penetrated the overwhelming darkness of the great woodland, casting only a faint glow on the railing and steps of the porch. Close by the light, leafy branches glittered and shifted.

"There's an outdoor light in the back too," Charlene said cautiously. "You go turn that on. At least we can see them if they try to come closer to the house."

I felt my way back through the dark living room. It was still unknown territory to me. I felt my leg brush the side of a chair, but I made it to the kitchen without tripping over anything.

"The switch is by the stove," Charlene called after me softly.

I stood by the kitchen window a moment, staring into the darkness. Through the trees, though I couldn't see it, I knew the lake was lapping mysteriously against the sandy shore. I thought if there were a moon I could see the water glistening between the trees. What I saw instead was a furtive shadow at the edge of the path to the lake, closer to the house than before. They—he—whoever it was, was moving in slowly, but surely. And now someone was around at the front of the house too.

I pushed the switch and a light went on at the far end of the yard. It wouldn't light the path all the way to the pier, but it was a help for someone walking back to the house after dark. Maybe Charlene and David went for romantic strolls down to the lake in the evenings. I had a fleeting impression of what the quiet summer nights could be like there at the lake house under normal conditions, when there were no madmen lurking behind the trees.

I hadn't heard Charlene moving until she spoke to me from the kitchen doorway.

"Marjorie."

I turned from the window. I couldn't really even see Charlene, but I knew she was there in the doorway.

"You keep watch here in the kitchen," she said tensely. "I'll watch in the living room. I've got the gun. If they try to come toward the house, we can see them now. You call out if you see anyone coming close, and I'll come right back here. Okay?"

"Okay." I tried to keep my voice steady. I didn't particularly want to stay alone in the pitch-dark kitchen, peering out the edge of the window to see if whoever was outside was going to try to get into the house. But there wasn't anything else to do now. It was useless to even think of getting to the car. We were trapped.

I didn't want to think about the newspaper story, but I had plenty of time to think and the story sat in my mind like a rock.

The time was unbearable. I lost all track of it. The minutes were hours long. Had the light intimidated whoever was crouching in the trees beyond the kitchen? Nothing moved in the fringe of the woods.

I thought we would have to stand guard by our windows all night long—and then unexpectedly Charlene called me in a hushed, urgent tone.

"Marjorie, come here—"

She sounded panic-stricken.

I fumbled my way across the dark living room toward the glimmering square of window where I could see Charlene standing.

"Listen—over at the side of the porch—" She strained toward the window, but the side porch was out of the range of our vision.

"Listen—" she whispered again. She had hardly said the word when I heard the creak of the steps and then the sound of footsteps on the porch.

"Quick, see what's happening in the back!" She drew away from the window to face the front door, holding the gun.

I turned to go and bumped into a small table which skidded back against the wall with a dull thud—just as I heard the sound of a hand at the door, turning the knob.

Paralyzed with fear, I stood rooted to the floor, while before my horrified eyes the door swung slowly open.

A figure stood outlined in the faint light of the lamp across the yard, and Charlene fired point-blank. And then fired again and fired again and fired again.

Chapter Fourteen

THE FIGURE CLUTCHED AT THE DOOR frame and then crumpled to the floor.

My own pulse hammered in my ears. I thought if my heart beat any harder it would explode. It was like the time I thought my lungs would burst in the swimming pool at school.

Charlene moved forward slowly, with her gun still pointed at the figure in the doorway. She leaned forward a moment, over the body. Her golden hair swung about her shoulders as she bent her head down to look.

With the door open, pale light from the outdoor lamp spread across the floor to where I still stood throbbing with every heartbeat, unable to move.

Charlene straightened up and looked back into the living room. When she saw me standing rooted in my spot she beckoned to me frantically.

"Come on! Now's our chance!"

When I continued to stand there, she ran to me and seized my arm and managed to haul me along after her, past the dead body in the doorway.

I knew, somehow, that it was a dead body. The police report later didn't surprise me about that. I think I will always hear those four ringing shots as Charlene fired. Who could survive such an onslaught?

I stumbled as she pulled me after her down the porch steps and across the grass toward the stairs to the road. I felt disorganized and clumsy and terribly, terribly afraid. My feet moved with the heaviness of a nightmare.

I was dizzy as Charlene gripped my arm more tightly and pulled me down the wooden stairs. The lamp cast light on the stairs and the road below. Our shadows sprang out ahead of us.

I remember thinking how large our shadows looked, plunging down the stairs while the tree branches glittered and shifted around us.

A timeless peace gripped the woods, as if to show a contrast to the struggle and terror of our affairs. At the car Charlene dropped my arm and reached into her skirt pocket for the car keys. She kept glancing back up the steps to see that we were not being followed. The key wouldn't go into the lock, and I watched, hypnotized by the desperate movement of her hand.

"Damn—damn—" She spit the words out with fury, and I looked once at her face. Her hair fell across her forehead; her eyes, lowered to the lock, were hidden from sight; but there was the emotion of crisis in every move she made.

"Damn—damn—damn—" The key raked against the lock with the grating sound of metal against metal.

I felt as if I were carved out of iron, as rigid as the lamppost at the head of the stairs.

The car door was flung open at last, and Charlene slid across to the driver's seat. "Get in—get in!" she called to me, jamming the key into the ignition.

When I didn't move at once, she shouted again. "Get in—get in! What's wrong with you!"

Dimly, in the night shadows, I could see the reflection of light on the chrome of a second car, pulled in behind Charlene's. It sat there, silent, mysterious, secretive in the darkness.

Nothing was real anymore.

"Marjorie!"

The engine revved. I knew she would go without me if I didn't move from my trance.

I got into the car, surprised to hear my own ragged breathing, surprised to feel a tightness in my throat from trying to hold back the tears of fright.

I felt tortured by the strain of the awful time watching at the kitchen window.

The car lunged forward and we sped off on the road that curved and wound between the forest trees. There was no light but the headlights, no light in all that incredible blackness. I had never been in such a far, lonely place in the dark of night. There was only the road unwinding before us. Everything else was mystery and darkness.

"We'll go to Crossing," Charlene gasped out the words. Her hands were clenched on the steering wheel. Dashboard lights reflected on her desperate face. She drove too fast for safety on the narrow, twisting road. She leaned forward, as if that could help us reach our destination even more quickly.

I sat with my hands twisted in a painful grip, my eyes magnetized to the road sweeping ahead in the glare of the headlights. I thought at any moment we might swerve and crash against a tree, so wildly did the woods flash by on either side.

On and on we went through the lonely night.

Racing from the lake house and the dead body in the doorway.

Chapter Fifteen

THERE WAS A SENSE OF UNREALITY ABOUT everything that had happened and was happening.

It seemed as if we drove forever.

But at last the lights of Crossing came into view.

So much had happened in the short time since we had been there earlier that evening. The peaceful streets appeared as if out of a dream, with no connection to any part of my life. It was as though I had never been there. The bleak, gray-walled room of the police station where Charlene and I arrived at last was in another world from the one with the luxurious homes that we had driven past so leisurely in the afternoon, watching girls play croquet on a shady lawn.

* * *

Charlene told the story of what had happened in an hysterical outburst. After all, she had just killed someone.

"And you have no idea who these men were?" the police officer asked.

He was a thin, tired-looking man who kept smoking cigarettes one right after the other.

Charlene shook her head with an expression of anguish. "How could I know who they were? It was too dark to really see them. They were just suddenly out there in the woods, creeping around. And then—then—"

She buried her face in her hands.

It was very dramatic, and I watched with blank fascination.

"And this person you say you shot—you can't identify him either?"

Charlene shook her head desperately, without looking up.

"It was David," I said numbly, although nobody had asked me. I think I looked too traumatized to be worth talking to. I was huddled in the green plastic police station chair, hair falling in my face, tears I didn't even brush away trickling down my cheeks.

The thin, tired-looking policeman turned toward me. "What was that, miss? What did you say?"

The other officer with us, an older, solemn man, turned toward me too. I had a sense of the room around me, everybody waiting, looking at me. There was a large clock on the wall, like a schoolroom clock. A desk with a phone, scattered papers.

Oh, where was Sanderville? And my house? And my mom and dad? And Trixie? And Eddie Jackson? Where was my real life?

"What was that you said?" the thin policeman asked me again.

"It was David—David Kensington." I stammered over the words, but everyone could hear me now.

Charlene lifted her face from her hands and stared at me with an expression of true and complete astonishment.

"Who is David Kensington?" The policeman looked from me to Charlene and back to me again. I had become the center of attention. I felt everyone looking at me, and I burst into fresh tears. The older policeman came to my chair and awkwardly patted my shoulder. "Now take it easy, take it easy," he said.

I looked up at him through a blur of tears. I didn't have everything figured out—not by a long way. But I knew that the man Charlene had fired at was David, and I knew that when she had fired she knew it was David. He was not an unknown, dangerous intruder she had to defend herself against. She was expecting him to come through that door at exactly that time, and it was no accident that she had killed him.

Just before she fired she had said softly, "Goodbye, David."

Chapter Sixteen

AND SO, AT A POLICE STATION IN A TOWN
I had never heard of before that day, my visit with
my cousin Charlene came to an end.

It is early winter now. I've had my birthday; I'm
sixteen now. The trial concerning the murder of
David Kensington is about to begin.

I will be giving testimony at the trial. It will be
one of the most unusual things that will probably
ever happen to me in my whole life.

I can imagine the faces present in the courtroom:
Mom and Dad, who thought they were leaving me
in tender loving care while they had their wonderful
trip to Italy. Aunt Kate and Uncle Gerald, grief-
stricken. We always had good times in their brown
frame house in Sanderville. Christmas Eves.
Thanksgivings. Strangers live there now.

Who else will be in there in the courtroom? Charlene's friends from Larrimore Hills, the ladies of the luncheon? Maybe some of them will come to the witness box and say that Charlene was a perfect wife. I don't think it will matter. No one will believe them now.

It took a while to get everything sorted out, but the pieces are falling into place. The picture is forming. One of the first to testify will be David's lawyer. David had planned to ask Charlene for a divorce. He told his lawyer that he felt he had married too quickly after Rosemary's death. He and Charlene were not compatible.

The prosecuting attorney intends to prove that Charlene suspected David would divorce her and she was filled with hatred at his rejection of her, as well as fear that she would lose the luxurious lifestyle that she had enjoyed as his wife.

She worked out a plan to kill David, a plan in which my visit played a very important part. I was her witness to the anonymous letters and their effect on her. The murder was going to appear to be a ghastly accident caused by her terror that night, which was increased by the strain the letters had already created.

She had written the letters herself, typed them on a typewriter that could not be traced—a floor model in a store perhaps—and mailed the first one so it would appear on the first morning of my visit.

She had nothing to fear by saving the second

letter. It couldn't be traced to her and it was good proof that David was trying to kill her.

If her plan had succeeded, the anonymous letters would have remained an unsolved mystery and she could tell everyone, "I guess I'll never know who it was that wrote to warn me." She would have said it with convincing regret, she was such a good actress. She had fooled me completely from the moment she first said so innocently, "I've just received the strangest letter." What an act she had put on at the lake house, frantically dragging me down the stairway to the car.

On the stand, Charlene will say that she had no idea David would turn up at the lake house that night.

However, a business friend of David's will testify that David and Charlene had made perfectly ordinary plans to spend the weekend at the lake. David would be finished with his business and drive directly to the house. The friend had breakfast with David that Friday morning, and David had casually mentioned his plans. He added that he had to phone Charlene to tell her he would be arriving at the lake Saturday night instead of Friday night.

David was not usually talkative about his affairs, and Charlene gambled that he wouldn't happen to mention his weekend plans to anyone. It was a risk she was willing to take, and one she lost.

After she got David's call, Charlene faked a headache and put off our going to the lake until Saturday. The prosecuting attorney feels sure that her phone call to David the night we had the pizza delivery was a fake too. "I think she had her finger holding down the release button on the phone," he told me. "She wanted to establish more firmly in your mind that David was still on his business trip and there would be no possible reason to think it might be David standing in the doorway when she fired the gun."

Once we were at the lake, it was easy for Charlene to pretend to discover an intruder, to start me worrying. She had time to tamper with the fuses and cut the phone wires while I was getting the groceries from the car; time to make gouge marks around the door with a screwdriver while I was upstairs checking to see if the lights were working in the bedrooms.

The figures I had seen lurking ominously in the darkening woods as night fell were no more than shadows created by my own imagination, keyed-up by the article about the escaped mental patient which Charlene had purposely saved and left on the patio for me to see. A fearful sense of the unknown descends upon a woodland when night comes. Books and movies assure us that isolated places are fraught with danger after dark—and in the fading light I was sure I saw things that were not there. I was ready to believe there were *two* men in the woods behind the house. I *saw* the figure by the trees at the end of the porch when Charlene told me it was there. To me there were real figures crouching in the shadows waiting to spring on us! My feelings of terror will not soon be forgotten. But there was no one there at all, until poor David came. As I stood watch at the kitchen window, I had not heard his car arrive on the road below the house.

When I bumped into the table on my way toward the kitchen, Charlene heard the sound as the table struck against the wall and thought I was there. She had no idea I was still right behind her in the dark, close enough to hear her when the door opened and she said, "Goodbye, David."

I'm not sure of all the things that Charlene did as she was growing up, but I do feel that between the day she stole her best friend's boyfriend and the day she married David Kensington, other things happened that would seem bad and horrible if we knew about them. Even *before* Gwen Avery and her boyfriend I think there were things in Charlene's life that would surprise good people.

I would rather not know them. I already feel bad enough. I had always thought Charlene was so wonderful.

Things are not always what they seem. My early, adoring memories of Charlene are now gone forever. All that remains is the memory of her shadowy figure in a dark room at the lake house—firing the gun and then again and then again and then again.

* * *

There is something else. No one has thought of this so far, except me. At least no one has thought of it that I know of. Maybe at the trial it will come up.

If it doesn't, I will have to tell it.

This has occurred to me: that Charlene was driven by something much more than just the threat of divorce.

I remember the day some years ago when my mom told Dad and me that Charlene was going to a resort for a few weeks. Charlene had been living in Chicago just a little while then, and she wrote occasionally to tell her news.

I can hear my father replying cheerfully. "Oh, the hard life of these young career girls."

We were sitting in the dining room on a warm July night, and I thought how glamorous it sounded that Charlene was off to a resort. I was about twelve then. None of my clothes fit right. I hated math and the boy behind me who pulled my hair. I wanted a rock to crawl under and hide. But my beautiful cousin Charlene was going to a resort. She had a glamorous job in Chicago, and now she was going to a resort. She would lie on a beautiful beach in a beautiful bathing suit, like the heroine of a movie.

At that time I had so longed to be like my cousin Charlene.

Now, thinking back over all that has happened, I wonder if the resort she went to was Greenwood Lake? Or if anyone would remember if they were asked now, after all these years.

I think it was. I think it was Greenwood Lake and I think she met David and Rosemary there. I think she knew that Rosemary sometimes swam out to the raft in the morning. I think one morning Charlene was on the raft, waiting for Rosemary—to keep her from climbing up—until in a panic Rosemary turned and tried to make it back to shore.

Perhaps, watching her, Charlene said softly to herself, "Goodbye, Rosemary."

It had happened so long ago, and apparently no finger of suspicion ever pointed to Charlene. Maybe we can never know exactly what happened the morning Rosemary drowned; but I think I know. I think Charlene had risked too much to get David, to accept the idea of divorce.

She had murdered to be his wife, and she wouldn't let him get away alive.

ABOUT THE AUTHOR

CAROL BEACH YORK started writing twenty-five years ago and her books have been universally acclaimed. She has authored over fifty books for all age levels, from beginning readers through young adults. Her books have been continuously in print; among them are the popular *Butterfield Square Stories* for younger readers, as well as *Nothing Ever Happens Here,* a novel for young adults. *Nights in Ghostland* will be coming from Archway Paperbacks in the fall of 1987. Ms. York grew up in Chicago, where she currently lives with her daughter. She is a favorite with librarians across the country who frequently recommend her books when a child is looking for a scary story that rings true.

HAVE YOU SEEN
NANCY
DREW°
LATELY?

Nancy Drew has become a girl of the 80's! There is hardly a girl from seven to seventeen who doesn't know her name.

Now you can continue to enjoy Nancy Drew in a new series, written for older readers–THE NANCY DREW FILES.™ Each pocket-sized book has more romance, fashion, mystery and adventure.

THE NANCY DREW FILES™

- # 1 SECRETS CAN KILL 64193/$2.75
- # 2 DEADLY INTENT 64393/$2.75
- # 3 MURDER ON ICE 64194/$2.75
- # 4 SMILE AND SAY MURDER 64585/$2.75
- # 5 HIT AND RUN HOLIDAY 64394/$2.75
- # 6 WHITE WATER TERROR 64586/$2.75
- # 7 DEADLY DOUBLES 62543/$2.75
- # 8 TWO POINTS FOR MURDER 63079/$2.75
- # 9 FALSE MOVES 63076/$2.75
- #10 BURIED SECRETS 63077/$2.75
- #11 HEART OF DANGER 63078/$2.75
- #12 FATAL RANSOM 62644/$2.75
- #13 WINGS OF FEAR 64137/ $2.75
- #14 THIS SIDE OF EVIL 64139/$2.75
- #15 TRIAL BY FIRE 64139/$2.75

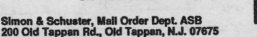

Simon & Schuster, Mail Order Dept. ASB
200 Old Tappan Rd., Old Tappan, N.J. 07675

Please send me the books I have checked above. I am enclosing $_____ (please add 75¢ to cover postage and handling for each order. N.Y.S. and N.Y.C. residents please add appropriate sales tax). Send check or money order–no cash or C.O.D.'s please. Allow up to six weeks for delivery. For purchases over $10.00 you may use VISA: card number, expiration date and customer signature must be included.

Name_____

Address _____

City _____ State/Zip _____

VISA Card No. _____ Exp. Date _____

Signature _____ 677